JT

JT

Front Cover

The top left picture is a younger JT, around the time when he used the alias "Mike Cassidy," a mentor to one who would become known as "Butch Cassidy."

The center picture is of JT after being grazed by a bullet during the Mexican Revolution, at the battle of the "Last Victory."

The top right picture is of JT in his retirement years, with his famous specially made Frontier Colt 44s.

The bottom left picture is of Pancho Villa with Ila and Marvelle, dressed as angels, accompanied by JT and a caravan of a dozen on their way to overthrow Porfirio Diaz at Ciudad Juarez and hand the presidency over to Madero.

The bottom right picture is of Pancho Villa, holding JT's son William's hand, at the battle of the "Last Victory."

Table of Contents

Introduction

John Todd (Tolliver) McClammy was born on September 5, 1868 in Dennards Bluff, Monroe, Alabama. Tolliver is a nickname for Todd that he liked to use. Later he was known mainly as JT. He was a wealthy rancher, realtor, mine owner, and for a short time, an outlaw of the late 1800s and early 1900s. On my last day with my grandmother, who we called Nana, I asked about her dad. I did not remember all the stories my grandmother had told growing up and wanted to hear the stories again before it was too late. My grandmother sat quietly on the couch. Looking at her face, I knew she was in deep thought, remembering her past. After a long pause Nana said, "My dad was quite the wild and free spirited cowboy when he was younger." Nana continued to tell the stories about Pancho Villa. "I knew Pancho Villa very well; I was there, I lived it." Nana spent all afternoon telling me about their adventures and some of the stories her mom and dad had told her. That was my last day with Nana before she passed away. Other chapters in JT's life before meeting the famous revolutionist, Pancho Villa are included here. Some of these stories are based on minimal facts. After thinking of how the events might have played out, the stories were manifested in dreams. The stories were exhilarating to write. Some say my great-grandfather channeled the stories through my dreams. The dreams I experienced felt very real, as though I was there. They were fun and exciting, and I felt compelled to share them. Regardless of their origin, the stories are historically based and are possibly the actual events. Some of the facts these stories are based on include a letter to Butch Cassidy's mother received while Butch was in prison. The letters that Butch wrote while he was in prison are said to be in the possession of a famous historian who has written books about the Hole in the Wall Gang. The letter is said to have been shown to a McClammy relative in Montana by this author for verification. The names have not been mentioned for privacy reasons. There is a rumor about a book in the process of being written by this author that can bring these facts to life. The letter tells how JT used the name Mike Cassidy when he was working at the Circle-K Ranch in Utah. During that time, a local cowhand was very impressed with his cattle driving and sharp-shooting skills. The young cowhand would become known to all as Butch Cassidy. Butch admired Mike Cassidy and considered him his mentor. History tells us that the cowhand, Roy Parker, was so impressed with his mentor Mike Cassidy that he later changed his name to George Cassidy. He was later given the name Butch from working in a meat plant, butchering cattle.

JT's sons, William, John, and George, after moving to Glendale, California, were known as the "Bad Boys of Glendale," and neighbor Marion Morrison, known to all as John Wayne, liked to hang out with the boys and play cowboys and Indians.

Charles Russell, who JT played poker with on occasion, painted many events of the times. Charles Russell's painting of a bear was a real story involving JT's brother Quincy.

Childhood dreams

Imagine living in Alabama in the mid-1800s. You are Will, young boy of eight years, the oldest of your brothers and sisters, living on a large plantation. Your family's black slave, who you call Nanny, comes in to wake you and your brothers for school. Your brothers complain that you kept them up most of the night by coughing. Nanny feels your head and tells you to come with her. Nanny tells you that you have a fever, and that she does not want you getting your brothers and sisters sick. Nanny tells Will to get his robe and to come down to the guest room while she informs the missus.

Nanny brings Mrs. Martha McClammy her toast and coffee and informs her of Will's condition. Mrs. Martha is alone in the bedroom. Mr. John McClammy has been up for hours, taking care of the business of running a large plantation. Martha tells Nanny to keep Will in the guest room until he is well and to make a cup of chicken soup for him and that she will have the doctor come by and look at Will today. The next day, Will's fever has broken and he is in the breakfast nook having his chicken soup and toast. The sun is shining in through the window on Will, warming him up as he looks out on a cold winter day. Will's father comes in from his office for a cup of coffee. Will sees this as a rare opportunity to talk to his father alone. "Good morning Father."

"Hi son. Eat your soup and get back in bed. We do not want to get your brothers and sisters sick again."

"I am feeling better, Father. I am going back to school tomorrow. Father, I have been wondering: have we always been plantation owners? Am I going to have a plantation like this one when I grow up?"

"Those are a lot of questions for a young lad. I have many important things I need to take care of; save it for another time when I am not so busy."

Will knew that would never happen. It seemed like his father worked all the time. His father never talked about family matters with the children. Mom was the one who did all the explaining to the children. Will was sad as his father walked away. These questions had been rolling around in his head for a very long time.

As his father walked away sipping his coffee, he turned and saw the sadness in his son's eyes. Will's father turned and said to Will, "I think I can take a small break. I have been working since early this morning, and it is time for lunch. Nanny, can you bring a bowl of soup and toast?"

"Yes sir, Mr. John."

John sat and sipped his coffee, looking at Will, wondering where the time had gone. Will was becoming a young man of eight. It seemed like yesterday he was a small boy yanking at his pant legs. John realized this was a good opportunity to have a father-son talk with his oldest son and to give his son dreams of a future to look forward to. "OK, Will, let us see about those questions now. Arriving from Scotland in the 1600s, generation after generation of McClammys have laid the ground with hard work and smart business. Your grandfather Mark McClammy is the wealthiest man in North Carolina, and as you can see, we are doing quite well ourselves. Keep up the good work with your schoolwork and learn the ways of the plantation by working the farm and livestock, and one day a plantation like this one can be yours."

"Father, will this always be our land, or can someone take it away from us?"

"Yes Will, there are those who want to change things and take our way of life away from us. There is a strong movement in the Union to free slaves, who we use to work our plantations."

"Father, what would we do without Nanny and her daughters to cook and clean our house and the other slaves that labor in our fields and care for our livestock?"

"Will, let us hope it never comes to that. The Union is suggesting equal rights for all and to free all slaves. Here at our home, we treat our slaves well. We give them a comfortable home and feed them well. We do not have anything to worry about Will; the Confederate army is strong and we have the wealth and political status to overpower the idealists of the Union. We will need to stay strong and fight hard for the tradition we have had for over 200 years." John knew he was becoming a bit carried away with his patriotism for the Confederacy. He told Will everything was fine and to go back to bed and rest.

John realized it was time to start teaching Will how to shoot long guns and pistols so that he could protect himself if something were to happen. John was quite the marksman and had a nice collection of guns. From that day on, John spent as much time as he could teaching Will how to shoot and defend himself. John knew the Civil War was coming, and he was going to do everything he could to keep Will alive.

The talk Will had with his father that day fueled his desire to become a wealthy plantation owner like his father. The conversation also infected him with anger and hatred towards the Union for trying to take his dreams away from him. Will practiced very hard at target practice with the long gun and pistols. He learned how the plantation worked and quickly became familiar with the slaves' duties. Alabama and Georgia were the first to provide cattle to the new Confederate States. The majority of the original cowboys were actually black slaves who wore big hats and cowhide boots. Will started at a young age, working with the cattle and riding horses with the black slave cowboys. After fattening them up, Will would help round them up and drive them to market.

Will's younger brothers were not as excited about being a cowboy as Will was. Will had fun learning how to ride and work the livestock. Will enjoyed going to school and was very good at schoolwork. He knew in order for his dream of being a wealthy plantation owner to come true, he had to be smart in business.

Will was closing in on his eighteenth birthday; he could almost feel the future he dreamed about for so long. Will tried to put the fear of war out of his mind and keep his dream alive, but every day the reality of the Civil War was coming closer. Will soon realized his boyish dreams were just that-dreams-and for the first time in his life, the future looked very scary.

Picking up the pieces

Standing center stage as the lovely and very young fifteen year-old Miss Mary Emma Snowden, who went by the name Molly, walked the aisle to become Will's wife, his mind wandered off as he looked down at the arm he lost in the war. Four horrifying years of war rattled around in his head as he tried to stay focused on the moment of getting married. Will and his dad John were in Company A, of Russell's fourth regiment, Alabama Cavalry. (The original Civil War registry was found in the *National Park and Service, U.S. Civil War soldiers, "1861-1865" database.*) His younger brother John was in the reserves. Will knew if his dad had not pushed him so hard, teaching him how to shoot, ride and defend himself, he would not be alive. The war was a bloody nightmare that he was desperately ready to put behind him.

Will knew this was a marriage of convenience during hard times. Molly was ten years younger than Will. Will remembered the day as a boy when his father told him how one day he would take his rightful place as a wealthy plantation owner with his own family. He looked up at Molly and told himself with new self-esteem, "I will pick up the pieces of this shattered life and build a new one." The ceremony continues and Will and Molly share their first kiss as husband and wife on January 5, 1865.

The first years for Will and Molly were the toughest. Most of the farms were destroyed and depleted of all livestock. Monroe, Alabama lay in ruins. This was definitely not the life Will dreamed about as a boy. He lived in the town of Monroe, Alabama on Beat 12 Street. He worked on his father's plantation, rebuilding it back into production. Many of the black slaves stayed on as laborers for food and housing. Other hired hands were white and black. Will helped manage the hired hands and was on his father's payroll.

He soon had a son, John, named after his father. This new addition to his life made him feel more complete, with the start of his own family. Will was eager to teach his son everything he knew. Molly and Will had five kids: John, Mark, Quincy, William, and Bettie. Will was very hard on John, never letting up. He knew this new United States would take a tough man to survive. He taught him how to shoot long guns and pistols. John practiced target shooting for long hours at a time. His dad taught him to work the plantation and to handle the livestock. This was always his dad's favorite. In the Civil War, Will was chosen to drive cattle to the north. This was a large source of income for the Confederate army. When John was a young man of twelve, Will sent him off on cattle drives in northern Alabama and Texas. Will had friends driving cattle after the war in northern Alabama and down through Texas. Will's goal was to toughen his son up any way he could. This usually appeared to others as being cruel and abusive.

Will and his son John worked at Grandpa John's plantation. The other kids were too young. Grandpa John bred prize-winning steers, thoroughbred horses and other livestock. The most sought after horse was the Irish Draught Warmbloods. These are powerful horses. The breeding technique was passed down from generation of McClammys by way of Ireland to Scotland. The large warmbloods originated from war horses brought to Ireland during the Norman invasion of Ireland and were bred with the local stock. They were later bred with Clydesdales, thoroughbred and half-bred sires.

On occasion, John would help on cattle drives. These cattle drives usually were just to bring the livestock to market or to the fair after fattening them up. The cattle drives to the north were something John experienced only a few times. Will had planned to give his other sons the same experiences and training that he had given John but unfortunate events prevented this from happening.

Will worked as a deputy sheriff in town. This, in his mind, helped keep the streets free of homeless and drunken ex–slaves, but really it was just a legal way to harass them. On a routine stroll through town as deputy sheriff, Will was shot and killed by a black man while trying to arrest him.

Will's stern hand in raising John made it possible for John to play the role of a man while still the age of a boy. John had already become known as a sharpshooter through local contests. John's horsemanship was known from winning many events in the local fairs. After Will's death Molly let John play the role of man of the house. This is how John coped with his dad's death. As John rode down the street riding his dad's horse and wearing his dad's guns, he was looked upon as a man, not a twelve year old boy.

The outlaw days

Soon after Will's death Molly remarried to Charles Payne. He was a very good man. Charles was a loving and kind father to his children, as well as to the McClammy kids. Molly and Charles had a daughter together, Kate. Molly was very much in love with Charles and was ready to start her new life. Molly started using her middle name, Emma. The McClammy kids were happy for their mother. They knew how mean their dad was. They all loved him, but at times, his bitter hatred of the world certainly took a toll on the family. They all moved to Bastrop, Texas, were Charles started his political career.

Soon after settling into their new home, the 1880 United States Federal Census was taking place. John was alone at home when the census taker knocked on the door. When the census taker asked John how old each member of the household was, John asked why. The census taker told John that this was a federal document of the citizens of the United States, documenting the number and age of its citizens. John knew he would need identification showing he was older than twelve years old to get hired on at the local ranches. John told the census taker that he was 18 years old. After the taker was done John received a copy of the document and used it to get hired on at a local ranch. The *1880 United State Federal Census* shows John as eighteen years old. John was born in 1868, making him only twelve years old in 1880.

Around the year 1882, John hooked up with a cattle drive that would take about six months. The drive would take him from Mexico to Montana. Early on, John had proven himself with the cowboys on the drive, with his fast draw and sharpshooting skills. The cowboys on the drive took a liking to John. Soon they were a tight working team of drivers. Most of the men had been with this group for two or three drives. One night at camp, a few of the men that had been teaching John some of their tricks of the trade asked him to sit with them. They wanted to discuss a plan of theirs with him. They were planning a bank robbery, and they wanted John's sharpshooter skills to frighten everyone in the bank into letting them have the money. They told John there was fifty thousand dollars, and one-fifth would be his. John did not want to be caught and go to jail. The cowboys repeatedly assured him of their success. They explained how they knew the bank's routine. They knew when the money transfer would take place and how many tellers would be in the bank. John did not want to turn on his new friends, so he said yes.

The next day, they misled the foreman into thinking they were going to a different town than the one they were robbing. When they left the area where the cattle were grazing, they turned south until they were out of sight. John was very nervous about the whole idea of robbing banks, but probably told himself that these guys had a good plan, so that he would calm down a bit. When they arrived in town, the bank robbery went just as planned. They put longhair wigs and big cowboy hats on. The plan was to look like the Jesse James gang. They called John Jesse and one of the other cowboys Frank. They rode different horses from camp so nobody would know who they were if seen later. During the robbery, John shot the guns in the holsters of two men in the bank. The cowboy they were calling Frank said, "Good shooting, Jesse."

He was so fast with his pistols, and when the people in the bank heard Jesse, it scared the crap out of them, and they dropped their guns on the floor. The cowboys knew the safe would be full of money from the delivery made by the stagecoach. The bank tellers loaded the money in saddlebags. They got away clean, without anyone on their trail. Afterwards, John was wound up from all the excitement of the robbery. John saw nothing but misery in his life up to this point and was not feeling any remorse. John told himself this was a chance to make some quick money and start a new life. The cowboys' planning of the robbery the year before paid off quite well, letting them get away incognito.

As the cowboys departed in different directions, one of them gave John a tip on a ranch in Utah needing ranch hands. He told John to tell him Wilson sent him. John said, "But who is Wilson?"

"Just tell the foreman when you get there. It would also be a good idea to change your name."

John decided to take their advice and head to the Circle-K ranch in Utah. They had not steered him wrong yet, and he had a saddlebag of money to prove it.

Bad influence leaves a name

John took his time riding to Utah, thinking of an alias to use. John pondered the idea all the way through Utah. He thought of shortening his name to JT. He liked the way that sounded, but it was a bit too obvious. He then remembered a classmate by the name of Mike Cassidy. He was the meanest kid in school and everyone was afraid of him. That would be his alias while in Utah working on the ranch. John rode into the town of Circleville late and checked into a room in town under the name of Mike Cassidy. He soon became comfortable using the name. *This was easy*, he thought. No one asks questions. You say you are a certain person, and you are.

After breakfast the next morning, he headed out to the Circle-K Ranch. When he was within a quarter mile of the ranch, a couple of riders came out to greet him. John reminded himself as he was riding up to them that he was Mike Cassidy.

"What is your business here?' asked one of the men, with his hand close to his pistol.

"I am here for work; Wilson sent me."

"Wilson?" said the man with his hand ready to draw on JT. "We do not know anyone by that name.

We are not hiring now. You best turn around and head on out."

The other cowboy rode close into his partner and told him to back down; that he had this one. "Wilson, you say. Come on, ride in with me. I will bring you to who you need to speak with."

JT was thinking to himself, *What have I gotten myself into?* as he rode with the men to the ranch house.

"Have a seat; he will be right with you."

JT was nervous. He had been thinking of this moment all the way from Montana. He had started to turn around and not make the trip two or three times. As he was sitting waiting for the foreman, he was wishing he had turned around.

After a while, the ranch foreman walked in and introduced himself. "Hi, I am Ed. Do you have a name?"

"Mike Cassidy," said JT.

"Good, you listened to Wilson and found yourself an alias. OK, Mike Cassidy, I have a problem with some local ranchers. What I want you to do is round up their strays at night and bring them into the branding stable. There will be a man there to take over from there."

JT spoke up. "That really was not what I had in mind for work."

The foreman told JT that Wilson sent word of one the best cattle drivers he had ever seen. "I need someone who could do this in the stealth of the night and not get caught. Now, is that someone you? The owner will pay you very well. He wants to send a message to the local ranchers."

JT asked how much he was paying for this risk. "If I'm caught, they could hang me."

"True, they could. Stay for two months and he will pay you two thousand dollars."

"Make it five thousand and I will do it." JT told himself if he got away with this, he would head back to Texas and would get out of the bad guy business for good.

Ed told JT, "OK I can authorize the five thousand, but there is one other thing I would like you to do. There is a kid from one of the neighboring ranches. Their family is very poor and the owner feels sorry for them. He has given their son a job. He is a hard worker and needs to be shown the operation of a cattle ranch. Bring him with you on your little errand and teach him a thing or two."

JT did not see how the work he is doing could be a good influence on anyone.

A few weeks went by and JT was actually having a good time showing off his quick draw to his new sidekick, Roy. He brought Roy along with him on his slanderous duty of cattle rustling. This part of the job JT was not having fun with, although Roy did not have much of a problem with the dirty business. After a while, JT felt comfortable with Roy and told him stories of his last cattle drive and the robberies. JT was going by the alias of Mike Cassidy, so what harm could it do, although JT slipped and used his real name a few times when telling his stories. Roy just said, "That is OK, Mike, I understand."

Roy ate up every word JT told him. He thought JT was the greatest. About a month or so went by and the neighboring ranches were catching on to the missing cattle and were setting up ambushes at night. JT and Roy almost rode right into one of the ambushes. As JT and Roy were getting ready to snag a few cattle out in the pastures, three men rode up behind them and caught them off guard.

"We caught them!" one of the men shouted as his gun was pointed at Roy and Mike.

Roy spoke up quickly. "It is me, Roy Parker. Ed sent us out looking for our strays before someone stole them, because of all the cattle rustling going on."

"OK Roy, maybe next time bring a lantern so you can see what you are doing."

"Yes sir. Good luck catching the rustlers."

JT thanked Roy on the ride back to the ranch. "That is OK, Mr. Cassidy. After everything you have done for me, I owed you one."

JT told Roy, "I will probably be headed out in the morning; it is getting to be a little too risky around here." In the morning JT settled with the owner and started his journey home to Texas. JT never used the name Mike Cassidy again.

Thanks for saving my scalp

JT headed north from Utah, taking his time on the way back to Texas to see his family. He was feeling remorse for his unlawful actions and made a decision right then and there to become a law abiding citizen. While feeling some remorse, he was also feeling pretty darn good about all the money he had acquired. JT was carrying around twenty thousand dollars with him and feeling cautious; pistols and long gun were loaded and ready to fire if needed.

JT heard of a ranch in Montana called Bar-11. It was said that if a drover with good horseman skills could be hired on there, he could do very well for himself. After leaving the Circle-K Ranch in Utah, JT made the trip to the Bar-11 ranch in Montana to inquire about work. After JT spent a day at the Bar-11 ranch, showing off his cutting and roping skills, the foreman let him know that any time he made it back this way, he had a job waiting. JT said he would take him up on his offer and would see him in a couple of months. JT was on the right track. Knowing he had a good job waiting made him feel good about himself again.

JT decided to travel through the western states and swing back around through California, Arizona, and New Mexico on his way home to Texas. He was missing his mom, brothers and sisters and was looking forward to being with family. Riding by himself, he was at risk of an ambush by hostile Indians or cowboys, so he had his pistols and long guns fully loaded and at his side at all times. There was no way he was going to let anyone take his money. JT had a nice, peaceful trip, stopping from town to town, taking the time to have a nice dinner, play a little poker, enjoy himself a bit and move on.

A few weeks or so into his trip, JT was riding through Arizona. As he rode over a small hill on the trail, he heard gunfire. JT saw, to his surprise, a man being chased by what looked like Apache Indians. JT, already traveling vigilantly for days, with his guns ready to shoot something, sprang into action, racing toward the Indians. With his long gun he picked off a few Indians. As he rode closer, both JT and the other cowboy shoot two six shooters, luckily hitting what they were shooting at, because there were better than twenty-five Indians shooting arrows and guns.

JT was hit three times with arrows, twice in the back and once in the leg. The other cowboy was hit a few times as well, once in the back and once in the arm, and his horse was killed. They managed to kill enough Indians to make them scatter. JT rode towards the other cowboy and told him to get on his horse and so they could get out of there.

"I will leave the saddle, but I need my bags." He quickly grabbed his bags and jumped onto JT's horse.

They were both bleeding pretty badly, but luckily most of the arrows hit at an angle and did not cut too deeply, except for one that hit the other cowboy's arm and ripped straight through. JT was riding fast, and the cowboy on the back told JT to cut across the hills ahead; it was a shortcut to a trail to Phoenix. There was no time for small talk. JT kept riding hard while his passenger was looking out for Apache Indians. Both JT and his new friend were sure the Indians had not given up. The Indians that had scattered most likely went back for reinforcements. JT rode hard and fast, knowing there could be hundreds of Indians returning to hunt them down.

They rode for about a half hour before the cowboy riding on the back of JT's horse said to JT, "Thanks for saving my hide."

JT said, "You mean scalp."

JT's new friend said, "You are right; we are lucky to have our scalps. I am Frank. Thanks again, I owe you big time."

"Let us get patched up before you thank me too much."

"We will make it, JT. Straight ahead, in about an hour, we will be in Phoenix."

They made it to Phoenix and got themselves patched up. Frank insisted JT stay at his house to recover. The doctor had them pumped up with morphine most of the first week, so they were feeling no pain. Frank had a very nice home with hired help to maintain his spread. Frank was much older than JT but it was not as noticeable to others. JT had matured quickly in the last year and looked twice his age. Frank and JT swapped stories and joked around as if they were old time friends. It was probably the morphine, although they certainly hit it off like two peas in a pod.

After about a week or so, they took the buggy into town. They had to get out of the house; they were both feeling a bit stir-crazy. Riding through town, they were stared at and greeted by the locals. What they did not realize is that they had already become a legend in the eyes of the townsfolk.

"Come into the saloon and tell us your story," one of the locals shouted as they rode by.

Frank said, "Not today, partner; we have business to take care of."

JT said, "We do?"

"Yes JT, let me show you what I was doing out in the middle of nowhere."

JT saw the sign on his office: Real Estate and Land Surveying.

"Real estate is the best investment you can make, JT. I was out surveying land of the Indian territories for the government. I need the money for land I am going to purchase in Tucson. That is why the contents of the bag were so important. The survey papers represent a month of surveying and are worth about five thousand dollars."

JT noticed a map on his wall with properties marked all over it. Frank told him, "Those are the properties I have for sale. These others are properties I am selling for my clients. I am a real estate broker, as well."

JT said, "I did not realize my new friend was so rich."

Frank explained, "It looks good on paper, but I need to turn some of these properties into cash before I can purchase the land in Tucson. Then I will be rich when that part of the town is developed."

JT told Frank, "I have been looking for good investments. Can I invest in any of these properties?"

"For saving my life, JT, I will give you property."

"Frank, show me your trade and that will be gratitude enough."

Frank told JT about his business and how to acquire a broker's license. He told JT that if he wanted to work for him, he could pay him well. JT told Frank he was a drover and had a job waiting for him in Montana on a prosperous cattle ranch.

There was a knock on the door; it was a telegram from a client who wanted to buy one of his properties. Frank told JT he needed the money to purchase his Tucson land and needed to go meet the client. Frank told the messenger to wait while he responded.

JT interrupted and told the messenger boy to come back in an hour. Frank was a little disturbed by this and told JT he needed to respond to the telegram. JT asked Frank to let him explain. Frank said OK and told the messenger boy to come back in an hour. JT asked Frank, "How much money are you short on the Tucson property?"

"About ten thousand. I need to sell about ten of my properties."

JT said, "That must be a lot of land for that much."

"It is, JT, and it can be subdivided into smaller commercial lots worth a hundred times my original investment."

"Frank, I have been saving money for a few years now, and I want a good place to invest it. I do not trust banks, and it has been making me very nervous carrying it around for the last month."

"JT, you have had money with you all the way from Montana?"

"Yes Frank, I have. It is in my saddlebag in your locker at your house. I checked before we left, and it is still all there."

"How much are we talking about, JT?"

"A little over twenty thousand dollars."

"JT, you are making me nervous now. Let us head back to the house; we can talk on the way."

While riding back, JT tells Frank that he trusted him with his life, and he knew he could trust him with his money. "I know I will get a good return on this money by letting you use it on your Tucson property. We will keep in contact by mail, and I should make it down this way about every six months."

"JT, you have my word. I will not let you down. I will make you rich one day."

JT handed Frank ten thousand dollars in cash and shook hands on it. JT was actually relieved that he did not have to carry all that money around anymore. JT knew he was doing the right thing, and by doing so created a trust and bond of friendship. A couple of days later, JT packed up his horse and headed toward Texas to see his family that he had not seen in over a year. After a nice visit, he told his mom that he had met with the Bar-11 ranch foreman, located outside of Great Falls, Montana. He had a job lined up as a drover when he returned. The cattle drives would take him through Texas, and he would get to stop back in for a visit in about six months.

Before leaving Texas, JT rode into El Paso to look for properties for sale, now that this idea of making money by buying real estate was rolling around in his head. There was a housing development outside of town. They had pictures and drawings of houses you could have built. JT was excited about the idea and knew he still had money in his bags, about ten thousand. JT put money down on a two-story house that had not been built yet. JT thought this would work out perfectly. He would not be back until it was built, and he could always sell the house and make a good profit. After his real estate dealings in El Paso, Texas, he made his trip to Great Falls, Montana.

The sheriff

The Bar-11 ranch was located just outside Great Falls in a town that would later be called Shelby. JT fit in right away at the Bar-11 ranch. He became well liked and respected for his talents as a cattle driver and his lightning fast draw with dead-on accuracy.

The Bar-11 ranch drove large herds that ranged from three thousand to five thousand head of cattle through the Chisholm Trail. The trail stretched from Mexico to Montana and was some of the harshest land on earth, as well as some of the most majestic. Part of the trail in the northern territories was also known as the outlaw trail. JT wondered if he would come across any of the cowboys he had ridden with on his earlier drive through that territory.

About every six months, JT would visit his family and then his friend Frank in Phoenix. Frank's investments were going very well. Frank was an honorable friend who kept his word. Frank had set up investments for JT, such as mines and property in Mexico and Phoenix, and repaid him in full. JT and Frank had become very good friends. When JT would visit, they would go into town, reminisce about their shootout with the Indians, play poker, and have a great time enjoying all that the town had to offer.

JT had been with Bar-11 ranch for many years and had just completed a drive through the Chisholm Trail. Halfway through the drive, JT was made foreman. All the cowboys working for Bar-11 knew of JT's excellent cattle driving skills. When the foreman had to leave unexpectedly during the drive, JT was undisputedly chosen to become foreman. After returning from the drive, JT was officially made foreman of the Bar-11 ranch. He then planned for a good meal, hot bath, shave and a good night's sleep at his hotel room in Shelby.

As he entered the hotel, he was welcomed back by the manager, who informed him of an outlaw named Frank Murphy, who was wanted for murder and horse theft. The local sheriff left a message with the manager for JT. The sheriff had summoned JT to join the posse after Murphy. JT asked the manager to send a message to the sheriff, informing him that he had just returned from a long cattle drive, and that if the matter became urgent, to send someone to wake him, and he would join the posse. He really did not want anything to do with a posse. JT could now get a good night's sleep. In the morning, he would hear that Murphy was captured, and that would be the end of the story. JT dozed off into a deep sleep for a few hours and was awakened by the telegraph operator pounding at his door. JT had told the sheriff to wake him if he heard any news, not thinking for a moment he actually would.

"What is it?" shouted JT. He was abruptly awakened and was very grouchy.

The telegraph operator replied, "I just received a wire from the depot agent at Conrad. Murphy just killed another man. He is headed for the construction camp nearby."

JT shouted out a loud grunt and let the telegraph operator in. "I will have to go kill that bastard myself, so I can get some sleep."

The telegraph operator handed a sheriff badge to JT and told him Sheriff Clary wanted him to have this to assure everyone on sight of his authority. Memories of JT's dad, who was shot and killed by a black man while trying to arrest him as deputy sheriff, briefly came to surface. He brushed off the eerie feeling and told the telegram operator to rush to the hardware store and collect as many 30-30 shells as he could carry. JT fitted out as fast as he could and grabbed his long gun and the 30-30 shells. He barely caught the freight train out of town to Conrad.

Upon arriving in Conrad, he was quickly told the details of the coldblooded murder. Murphy's horse had been driven into the dirt and left outside of town. He hid his saddle in a nearby stable. JT told the other deputy sheriff that he figured out what Murphy's plan was: he was going after a fresh horse. JT moved in slowly to see if he could spot Murphy. JT saw some movement in one of the tents, and then a black man came running out. Murphy had told the black man to go kill the man across the way and steal his horse. While the black man was running across the camp, JT snuck up behind Murphy and slammed his long gun down on him. Murphy fell to the floor. JT shoved his long gun against the back of his head and told him, "Please make a move, so I can blow your head off."

JT tied him up real good and gagged him. He could not stand hearing him whine anymore. JT dragged him onto the back of a mule and brought him into Fort Benton to Sheriff Tom Clary. The sheriff was extremely grateful for the fine deed JT had done. Sheriff Clary told JT he did not have reward money. All that he had in his possession were two specially made single action Frontier model Colt 44 pistols. He obtained them from a gunslinger who came into town and picked a fight with the wrong person. The pistols had remained in his safe unclaimed to this day. The sheriff expressed to JT that he did not think these pistols could find a better home and he would like him to take the pistols for a job well done.

JT conveyed his thanks to the sheriff and told

him he had not seen this kind of craftsmanship since he was a boy. JT's Grandpa John had a collection of the finest pistols made at the time. JT marveled at the pistols for a few minutes and told Tom that he thought these might be the finest pair of pistols that he had ever laid his eyes on. JT thanked the sheriff again for his reward and took the train back to Shelby. JT was treated as a hero back at the Bar-11 ranch. He ate it up and had fun showing off his new six-shooters.

The Big Die-Up

Many years had passed from the day JT started with the Bar-11 ranch. JT was just eighteen years old. The owner of the Bar-11 ranch had been made to believe he was close to twenty four years old. The winter of 1886-1887 put JT's cattle-driving skills to the ultimate test.

The summer of 1886 was one of the hottest ever. Streams and water holes dried up in Mexico and throughout the Southern Territory. This was the toughest drive JT had ever experienced. Fall approached as they entered the Northern Territory, and the cattle had not been fattening up. JT had received word that the public grazing pastures of Montana were dried out, and many brush fires filled the state with a black smoke that darkened the sky. To make things worse, there were a record number of new cattle companies driving their cattle into the Northern Territories with anticipation of green pastures for fattening up their stock.

JT remembered a canyon that he had made camp in one night. There were drawings on the walls from an extinct tribe of Indians that had lived there at one time. He remembered the drawings vividly because they were so large. The message in the drawing must have been very important, so they sat around the camp trying to figure out their meaning. The drawings had fiery fields and black skies. Then they showed the pastures covered with snow. The last picture was of dead buffalo everywhere. JT realized that what the Indians drew about long ago was happening right now to them.

JT recalled how they fed the stock in Alabama on Grandpa John's plantation. There were no public grazing areas in the South. Hay was grown and brought to fatten up the stock. JT knew this story would sound crazy to the owner of the Bar-11 ranch, but he had to send a telegram and try. The owner of the Bar-11 ranch trusted JT and decided to take his advice. Many of the local ranches, including Bar-11, had already placed their orders for hay for their fenced-in stock only. It seemed absurd to try to feed thousands of cattle with hay bales instead of grazing on public pastures. The owner of Bar-11 purchased as much hay as he could from neighboring states.

The winter unfolded just as the Indian pictures had shown. Thousands of cattle were frozen. Many cowboys were also found frozen. JT and the cowboys of the Bar-11 ranch worked fiercely in brutally cold conditions that lasted over one hundred days. They rounded up their cattle and kept them separate from the other brands. This was very difficult on public pastures, under these extreme cold conditions. They brought in bundles of hay by the wagonload. They kept the cattle crowded together to keep them from freezing. After the hundred days of freezing conditions, they had lost less than fifty cattle. The owner of the Bar-11 ranch was grateful for JT's insight on the brutal winter they had endured. For JT's hard work over the winter, he was promoted to manager of the Bar-11 ranch in 1888. After the snow had melted, the fields were covered with thousands of dead cattle. They called it the "Big Die-Up."

A newspaper article found in *The Daily Tribune*, Salt Lake City, December 24, 1898 substantiates certain facts presented previously. The article reads as follows: *JT McClammy, the northern Montana cattleman who was arrested in Salt Lake last week on the order of the authorities of Teton county, spent Christmas in Helena, having arrived in the custody of Sheriff Hagen early yesterday morning. Mr. McClammy was only nominally in custody while in Helena, and seemed quite as anxious to return to Teton County as was the man who charged him with highway robbery. In the company of a friend, he called at the independent office last night and told his side of the story. "I am* charged with highway robbery," he said, "by a man who owes me money, and who lived at my expense for several months." He went on to say, "There is not the slightest foundation for the charge, and I anticipate no trouble at all in securing a dismissal of the case."

JT's charges were dropped as anticipated. The newspaper article continues and announces JT's good character: *Mr. McClammy is one of the well-known cattlemen of northern Montana. He was formerly General Manager of the Bar-11 Cattle Company, controlled by David G. Browne and Charles E. Duer, of Great Falls. It is said of Mr. McClammy that he is a remarkable expert with his six-shooter.*

Frank's wedding

Almost ten years later after being promoted to manager of the Bar-11 ranch, JT received a letter from his friend Frank that he was getting married. Frank wrote that he had been courting his sweetheart for a while now, and he proposed to her last month. They were going to tie the knot and asked JT to please come down and join them in the celebration. With the mail being backed up due to the winter storms, the letter arrived late. The wedding was in two weeks and JT had not responded. Frank had not heard from JT in seven months and probably was wondering what was going on with him. JT usually corresponded a few times during that amount of time.

JT had been caught up in his work, and now being the big ramrod, he was busier than ever with managing the Bar-11 ranch. After reading Frank's letter, JT was very excited to see Frank and his new sweetheart. The investments that Frank had purchased for him had only been pieces of paper for a dream of a future life. It was time for JT to go see what they all amounted to. JT explained to the owner of the Bar-11 ranch his situation and requested a leave of absence. JT and the owner were on very good terms. JT was told to take as much time as he needed, and they would see him when he returned.

JT did not have time to make a leisurely trip this time, so he took what trains were available, making his way to Phoenix, Arizona. This took about a week and a half. Many new railroads were under construction and some were just opening. This was due mostly to the California Klondike gold rush. The trip was chopped up between train and horseback. With careful planning and a little bit of luck, JT arrived a couple of days before the wedding.

Frank was at the Phoenix train station to greet JT. Frank was excited to see JT and told him everything that had been going on, especially all about Ila. Frank told JT how well all his investments are doing, and he would get into the details after the wedding. "First, you are going to meet Ila, the sweetest thing on this earth."

As they entered Frank's spread, men were waiting to take care of JT's horse and supplies. JT and Frank entered the house, and JT was greeted with a very warm welcome. Frank immediately introduced Ila, and they sat down to enjoy a few cold beers and conversation. Ila's anticipation of JT's arrival and the stories Frank had told her made her feel as if she had already met JT. On the other hand, Frank had told JT very little about Ila, but it really did not matter to JT. The only thing JT needed to know was that Frank was happy. After spending only a short time together with Frank and Ila, JT saw how great they were together and how sweet Ila was. They made JT feel a part of their family, giving him that warm feeling of being in a home and not just a house.

Over the next couple of days, Frank's house was transformed into a beautiful wedding chapel. JT helped Frank build some of the decorations. Ila insisted on it. Ila said it was a labor of love that transformed the room into a chapel of matrimony. While Frank and JT were working, Frank turned to JT and asked what he was doing.

"I am cutting the wood where you marked it."

While JT was not much of a carpenter, that was not what Frank meant. "What are you doing still working in Montana? You know you are on the way to becoming a very wealthy man. JT, I know you felt you had to work and accomplish certain things in your life before you could move on, so what is next? What does JT want to do?"

JT said, "I have my eyes on a ranch for sale in Montana. I would like to start my own cattle ranch. I have also been working with the owner of the Bar-11 ranch breeding thoroughbred horses. I am good at it.

I remember tricks my grandfather taught me as a kid and have a few new ones of my own."

Frank said, "So you want to buy a ranch and breed thoroughbred horses. I like that. Let me handle the real estate transactions for you. You have quite a bit of cash for seed money. You should have no problem accomplishing that dream."

JT said, "That is what I was hoping to hear."

Frank said, "Like I told you before your investments have done well. On the other hand, you could move down here. Work the real estate business and breed your thoroughbred horses."

JT said, "That does sound very appealing. I want to tell you I certainly like what you have. You have made quite the life for yourself and your wife to be, and I do not think you could have found a sweeter woman to be with than Ila. There is another reason for building a working ranch. I would like to bring my brothers with me this time to Montana. I hope to have them eventually run the ranch."

Frank says, "I do understand, JT. I have no doubts that you can make that happen. Now let us nail those pieces of wood together and build our wedding arch."

Frank and JT completed the wedding arch. It was painted white and ready for Ila to decorate. By the weekend, the house was ready for the wedding. As JT, Frank and Ila stood around looking at the room they converted into a wedding chapel, Ila asked, "Do you feel the labor of love?"

"Yes, we do," Frank and JT said at the same time, while shaking hands and getting a huge hug from Ila, who had a big smile with tears of happiness.

Later, a nice rehearsal dinner was served for all who helped. Drink and conversation with some of Frank and Ila's friends and neighbors finished off the day before the wedding.

The wedding day was spectacular. JT woke early as always and helped around the house with last minute details such as tables and chairs. About a hundred or so guests were expected. Outside accommodations for a buggy valet were being made. Additional posts were driven to tie off the horses. An early breakfast was served. Frank and Ila had breakfast in bed and were not seen until about two hours before the wedding. Frank had planned everything very well, and the house was ready for guests to arrive and begin the wedding. All were dressed in duds finer than those for Sunday church, and the house was decorated elegantly. The wedding ceremony went just the way Ila had dreamed it would go. This was noticeable by Ila's glowing smile and tears of happiness. Frank and Ila were pronounced man and wife and everyone clapped and cheered. There was a lot of love and friendship in the room.

Soon after, the reception began. The dinner was spectacular, and the atmosphere was filled with an elegant feeling of high class. A band played that included a very talented violinist. The bouquet was thrown and drink and dancing filled the evening. JT gave a toast along with about twenty other gentlemen throughout the night. The night was perfect and went off without a hitch--well except for the one. A *1900 United States Federal Census* shows Frank M. King married to Ila for three years and shows their residence in Tucson City (all south of Ochoa from 6th Avenue to city limits), Arizona Territory.

High times for the brothers

JT had written to his brothers letting them know he was coming down for his friend's wedding, and asking if they wanted to ride back with him and start work at the Bar-11 ranch in Great Falls, Montana. His two brothers, younger by ten and fifteen years, William and Quincy, wrote back saying most definitely, yes; they thought he would never ask. His brother Mark, just two years younger, asked if they could all visit relatives in Helena, Montana.

After receiving JT's letter from the month before, they had been waiting eagerly. Will and Quincy had been working hard and long hours for local cattle ranchers. They looked forward to being part of a long cattle drive. Mark had been waiting patiently as well to make the trip to Helena, Montana to visit his relatives. JT missed his brothers. He was very excited to spend time with them on the ride back to the Bar-11 ranch. He also missed his sister, Bettie, and was wondering how she was getting along. Before leaving, JT took his whole family out to breakfast in an upscale restaurant in El Paso. This included his stepdad Charles, stepbrother Robert and half stepsister Kate and, of course, his mom, brothers and sister. The family enjoyed conversation and each other's company. Emma told JT about Charles's political career. Emma wanted to show JT that Charles was in the newspaper almost every week. Emma was very proud of Charles. They flipped through the newspaper, where Emma showed JT articles of Charles's political achievements. JT told his mom that she had really come a long way, and he was proud of her. This made Emma feel very good about herself. JT had made his family feel a bit closer to each other. Although the family was taking off in different directions, there seemed to be a kind of peaceful bonding feeling that everything would be OK. Emma told JT thank you and told him what a kind gentleman he had become. The boys said their goodbyes, saddled up, and were on their way to Montana.

The trip to Montana gave the boys a chance to share their stories and get to know each other again. They arrived in Helena, Montana and were excited to visit relatives that they had not seen in many years. The boys were made to feel right at home. They enjoyed the hospitality for a few days before leaving for Great Falls, with the exception of Mark, who decided to stay in Helena.

The boys completed their trip to the Bar-11 ranch. Upon arriving, JT immediately put his brothers to work. JT set his brothers up with the foreman to see what kind of riders they had become. The foreman reported to JT that they were hard workers and they would be excellent ranch hands. JT said, "Thanks, keep up the good work."

JT was the big ramrod, and his brothers saw how well he was respected. It was time for JT to organize another cattle drive from Mexico to Montana for the Bar-11 ranch. JT had put off discussing his plan of starting his own cattle ranch for fear of how the owner would respond. JT knew the owner was a fair man and would do just about anything for him, but he was still apprehensive. As JT was doing paperwork and making his chart of riders and positions for the drive, the owner sat down and asked JT about his trip and how things were going. This was the opportune moment for JT to discuss his plans with the owner.

JT laid out his plans of owning his own ranch and how breeding thoroughbreds was a big part of his plans. To JT's surprise, the owner understood completely and offered to help him get started. The owner suggested that JT buy a couple thousand heads of cattle, drive them together with Bar-11's, and cut them out when he returned to Montana. It was no longer a dream; his plan was coming to life. Now he needed to wire Frank and have him go ahead and buy the property just outside Shelby. This was a prime piece of land for what he had planned. JT estimated it would take a few months to get his new ranch up and running.

The drive was set up and JT, his brothers and the other cowhands were on their way to Mexico to drive about eight to ten thousand cattle through the Chisholm Trail. This would be the largest drive ever attempted. A train and horses would get them there in about a week. On the trip, JT finally had a chance to tell his brothers of his plans to start his new ranch, and how he wanted his brothers to help him run it. His brothers thought it was a great idea and were as excited as JT about it.

After arriving in Mexico, it was time to start rounding up cattle. The cattle were purchased from five different ranches. The herd was so large they took trails going around all towns. A week into the drive, all the cattle were herded together and headed north up through the Chisholm Trail to the Bar-11 ranch, and two thousand head to JT's new ranch. At the end of a long day, as camp was being set up, JT rode up ahead and stopped at a ridge overlooking the valley where the cattle were settling down for the night. JT sat up there until dark, thinking about his brothers and how he wanted to be a good influence on them. He was determined to set them on the right track. He knew how easy it was to be misguided, and being on this cattle drive was the best place for them.

JT rode down to camp and sat next to his brothers with a plate of grub. They talked for a long while about the drive and the new ranch. Will and Quincy were feeling very good about the new life on the JT ranch; that is what his brothers were calling it. Before JT hit the sack, he told Will and Quincy he would meet up with them in a few days. JT told his brothers, "There is a small town just outside a large valley where we let the cattle fatten up. Come into town, and I will buy you a steak dinner."

JT wanted his brothers to have a good time in town and was riding ahead to set up the details. They were going to take advantage of everything this little town had to offer. A few days later, Will and Quincy came riding into town. They were looking forward to collecting on that steak dinner JT had promised. They checked at the hotel to see if he was in his room. When they arrived at the hotel registry counter, Will proceeded to tell the manager that their brother was staying here and before Will could finish his sentence, the hotel manager looked at the both of them and said, "You must be Will and Quincy. JT told us you would probably be riding in soon. Here are your keys to your rooms. He wanted me to ask if you had anything nice to wear."

Quincy said, "Just what we have on and another set just like it."

The manager said, "JT thought so. Go around the corner into the little clothes shop. They know you are coming. They will set you up with some fancy duds. After that, go across the street to the barber. He has a shave and a hot bath waiting for you. Then, when you are all done and gussied up, come back here and your escorts will be waiting for you to take you to dinner. I almost forgot, JT wanted me to tell you; if you do not hurry up, you guys will be buying the first two rounds of drinks."

Will and Quincy were grinning ear to ear, hooting and hollering all the way over to the clothes shop. They were all gussied up in no time at all. They eagerly made their way back to the hotel. As they opened the door to the hotel lobby, two lovely ladies skipped up to them, putting their arms around each of their arms, and asked, "Will you two gentlemen escort us to dinner?"

Will and Quincy said, "Gladly, ladies."

Will and Quincy arrived at JT's private dining room with the lovely ladies. JT said, "Sit down and have a drink."

"Thanks, brother," both of them said at the same time to JT.

JT said, "My pleasure. I have always wanted to

do this for my brothers, and here we are. Here is a toast: let this be the first of many nights on the town with my brothers."

The brothers and the lovely ladies had quite the perfect evening, just as JT had planned. After dinner, it was off to the saloon for dancing and more drinking. When it was late, they each headed back to their own rooms, accompanied by their lovely lady friends. JT met Will and Quincy for breakfast. JT was all packed, ready to head back to Shelby. JT gave a manly hug to both of them and told them he would see them soon, when it was time to cut out their two thousand head of cattle.

JT was eager to get back to Shelby. He wanted to make sure the ranch hands he had hired had completed mending the fence and completed the other items on his list. He wanted everything ready to drive his two thousand cattle to his new ranch. JT had cowboys ready to go to work to cut out the two thousand cattle from the ten thousand and herd them towards the new ranch.

When he arrived at JT ranch, he saw that everything had proceeded as planned. The cowboys he hired had done a fine job. They were hoping to be hired on permanently, so they wanted to impress JT. The arena and stables were prepared, and all that was missing now were his horses. The owner of Bar-11 Ranch had let JT use a stable. It was time to bring them to their new home. JT had thoroughbreds, quarter horses and his most sought after horses, the Irish Draught Warmbloods. JT's prize winning warmbloods derived from an age-old breeding technique that he had learned from his Grandpa John.

After a week, the house had a cook and five ranch hands and was fully stocked. Good timing, too. The next morning the herd was due to arrive. The two thousand cattle were cut out and brought to the ranch. JT set his brothers up with the business of the ranch and went over the list of buyers for their cattle. He sent Quincy to sell the cattle. After a few weeks, the cattle were sold and driven to their buyers at various locations. JT's ranch was up and running.

Feeling on top of the world

One afternoon, while on business and pleasure in Colorado Springs, JT had just finished an early supper at the local inn when he noticed an old newspaper on the wall, from 1894. As he read the article, the name Cassidy immediately caught his attention. He had not heard or read anything from the times of his excursions under the name of Mike Cassidy. JT was glued to every word. He had kept that experience a secret for a long time, and someone was letting the cat out of the bag. The article stated Cassidy was sentenced to two years in the state penitentiary after robbing the Telluride bank of $20,000. The interview told how the bank robber Butch Cassidy acquired his name. While cow punching at a ranch in Circleville, Utah, he met a cowboy by the name of Mike Cassidy, known only briefly as a fast drawing, fancy riding, no good son of a card shark, and Roy Parker called him his mentor and so honored him by using his last name. After reading that, JT's jaw dropped in amazement. JT completed the article and there was no mention of his real identity. JT was relieved. Apparently, no one knew Mike Cassidy's real identity, and that was the way JT wanted it.

The next day while buying supplies, JT had the

pleasure of meeting Buffalo Bill Cody. Mr. Cody caught a glimpse of his Colt 44s and proceeded to strike up a conversation with JT. "That is a pair of mighty fine looking pistols you're wearing there; I bet you have a story or two to tell."

JT recognized Buffalo Bill Cody and said, "As a matter a fact, I do, Mr. Cody."

Mr. Cody said, "You have me at a disadvantage--what might your name be?"

"JT McClammy."

Mr. Cody replied, "Nice to meet you," as they shook hands. Mr. Cody mentioned recalling stories told about a JT who had remarkable cattle skills in the big freeze and he understood he was a great marksman. He asked JT if he would join him for a drink a little later, that he would like to hear more of his stories. JT met with Mr. Cody that evening and told him most of his adventures, including one while riding through Arizona, assisting a stranger who was being attacked by fifty Indians, and how they just barely escaped with their scalps, but not before taking arrows in the back and arms and losing a horse.

Mr. Cody told JT these were great adventures he had lived, and he would like him to ride with him in tomorrow night's show, and tell his stories.

JT said, "It would be an honor, Mr. Cody."

Mr. Cody said, "Call me Bill, JT, and on stage call me Buffalo Bill. Come by the show in the morning and ride with me and you can show me how you make your horse dance."

JT was excited and feeling good about himself. He arrived at the show tents to find Buffalo Bill already working on the show. Mr. Cody rode up and said, "JT, good morning, good to see you are an early riser like me. As you can see, we have a bit of everything--barrel racing, roping and reining events. Do you see something that fancies you?"

JT said, "I would like to play around with all of them if I could."

Mr. Cody said, "JT, you go right ahead and play away."

"Thanks Bill, this looks like fun." JT showed off his horsemanship, roping, racing, reining, cutting; and of course his sharpshooting skills as he rode along shooting bottles off the wall. When JT was done, he rode over to Buffalo Bill. Buffalo Bill told JT how impressed he was with his riding and shooting skills and JT told Bill how much fun he was having in his playground and how it made him feel like a kid.

Mr. Cody said, "I really enjoyed watching you, JT, and it is great to see that wild spirit of a youth in you. JT, I would like you to be my guest of honor in the show. I have an artist that will paint our picture on our horses together for the show poster. This is going to be an exciting show, JT."

"Thank you for having me, Bill."

JT, it is an honor."

JT had the time of his life in the "Buffalo Bill Wild West Show." He had a poster with wild Bill Cody and was feeling on top of the world. JT's daughter Marvelle, who inherited the poster of JT and Buffalo Bill, was forced to sell it during hard times. The poster may be in the hands of a collector somewhere. With any luck, a copy will find its way home one day.

JT meets his sweetheart

While still in Colorado Springs a few days after his Buffalo Bill Wild West Show debut, JT was ready to head out of town. Riding down the street towards the stable where his Irish Draught Warmblood buggy horse was stabled, a very attractive lady on a black stallion caught his attention. It appeared that she was heading toward the stable, as well. JT arrived at the stables as the lady dismounted. JT tied her horse to the post and said, "Good day, Miss, my name is JT."

She said, "Yes, I know, I saw you in the show the other night. That was quite the performance. I am Julia."

"Well, Julia, it is a pleasure to make your acquaintance."

The stable hand greeted them and said, "Howdy folks, what can I do for you fine couple today?"

Julia replied, "No, we're not together. I have a buggy with supplies I ordered and my buggy horse."

"And sir, what can we do for you?"

"The same, actually--a buggy with supplies I ordered and my buggy horse."

"And you are sure you are not together?" he said laughingly. "OK let us start with you, Miss, what name do we have you under?"

"Miss Julia McGuire."

"And you, sir?"

"JT McClammy."

"Nice performance at the show."

JT said, "Thank you."

The stable hand looked at his paperwork and asked JT, "What kind of a buggy horse is that?"

JT told him that it was an Irish Draught Warmblood.

The stable hand said, "That's some powerful horse you have there. Well neither one of your orders has been completed. My brother went to a local ranch to complete some of the items; he should be back in a few hours."

JT said, "Thanks; we will see you a little later then." JT turned to Julia and said, "Julia can I buy you something cold to drink while we're waiting?"

"Why JT, yes you can."

JT and Julia visited the local tavern, away from the loud saloon occupied by the local whores and drunks. They sat and shared some wine and talked for many hours. Julia told JT about her adventure: She had just been on to the top of Pike's Peak. JT was very impressed and told her so. JT was intrigued by every word she spoke. Julia shared with JT her plans to work in real estate, and how she was trying to invest in property. JT mentioned how he also was investing in property and silver and copper mines, but how breeding thoroughbred horses had been the most enjoyable. JT shared some of his adventures, although he wanted to hear more about Julia than to speak about himself. They talked into the early night and shared dinner together; that then turned into a romantic evening that neither would ever forget. The following days were spent together before it was time to get back to their own worlds. They exchanged contact information in the hopes of seeing each other again soon.

Julia was ready to travel back to Kansas. JT had told Julia how he traveled through Kansas on his way from Mexico to Montana and would like to call on her when he came through next time.

Julia told JT, "You better," and added that she would be waiting for his letter to arrive by mail.

JT wrote to Julia and had the letter mailed before the first week went by. JT wanted to come to Kansas and see her. At the time, Julia lived with her mother, father, sisters, and brothers, so the visit had to be planned so that he was presented as a gentleman when introduced to Julie's family. JT made a very good impression on Julia's parents. He visited continuously over the next few months. JT knew this was the woman he wanted to spend the rest of his life with. He had been writing to Frank telling him of Julia and how he wanted to move to El Paso and live in the house he had built. JT had been renting the house out through Frank's real estate services. JT asked Frank if he could find the renters a new home and have the house furnished and decorated. Frank told JT not to worry; he would take care of everything. Frank insisted on having the wedding at his house, and they would live in the house in Phoenix until the El Paso house was ready.

The ranch was running smoothly and JT felt good about how his brothers had handled everything and knew they would be successful. The time was right; JT asked Julia to marry him, and she happily said yes. They were married shortly after at Frank and Ila King's house. The house was decorated like Frank's wedding was. The same arch they had built together was in place and the loving touch of Ila was present in the decorations.

The Kings, who could not wait to meet Julia, eagerly greeted Julia and JT. The four of them quickly became the best of friends, as though Julia was the missing puzzle piece.

The wedding went off without a hitch--except the one, of course. The band played and dancing and drinking continued late into the night. The wedding was announced in all the papers. The article spoke of a quiet wedding. The wedding was not very quiet, though. That was an inside joke, since the reporter who wrote the article was at the wedding. He had asked JT and Julia how they wanted the article to read. JT and Julia agreed they would say they had been sweethearts in school when they were younger and had moved away from each other. This was a good story that kept their relationship a respectful one. This made Julia very happy.

The newspaper article, dated January 28, 1901 and found in the *Tucson Star* and the *Arizona Republican* newspaper reads as follows: *A quiet wedding occurred Friday evening at the House of Frank King, the contracting parties being J. Todd McClammy, who came to Tucson about two months ago from Montana in search of a milder climate, and Miss Julia McGuire. Miss McGuire arrived in the city about a week ago, neither knowing of each other's presence in the city until they came across each other by accident. They had attended school together and were sweethearts in the days gone by. On Friday afternoon, a marriage license was issued and that evening they were married.*

Julia, Ila and Marvelle, El Paso, Texas 1903-1904.

Shown is a picture of my Great Grandmother Julia holding my Grandmother Marvelle and my Great Aunt Ila standing next to them. Notice their first daughter is named Ila, after their good friends Frank and Ila King.

JT's two story house El Paso, Texas

Pulling the buggy is one of JT's prized Irish Draught Warmblood horses.

The Tiger rides into the Wolf's den

After the wedding, JT was excited to get started with business at hand. He planned to breed thoroughbred horses and run his mine in Chihuahua City, Chihuahua, Mexico. A trip to Mexico with Frank and a client was planned to show property. This was a chance for JT to meet Frank's contacts, establish his mine, and ranch in Chihuahua City, Chihuahua, Mexico. The three of them started out on their trip at dawn. The client was a former sheriff looking for property to retire on. They all were fully armed with long guns and pistols loaded and close at hand. They had to travel through a dangerous territory filled with bandits. This would save them a day of travel. Frank knew the trails around the areas where the bandits live and assured JT and his client there was not too much to worry about.

As they came to a narrow path, they could hear riders talking in Spanish. All three men spoke Spanish but could not make out what they were saying. The sheriff pulled out his long gun and Frank and JT had their pistols at hand. Not to provoke a fight, they remained calm as they came around the bend in the trail and the five riders came into sight.

"Good morning," JT says in Spanish as the riders approach them.

"Good morning, gringos; you are a long way from home. What are you doing here in the mountains?"

JT and his two companions had no idea at the time that they were talking to the great Mexican bandit Pancho Villa, with a bounty of fifty thousand dollars on his head.

JT told them they were taking a short cut to show their client ranch property. JT's fine crafted Colt 44 pistols caught Villa's eyes.

"Very nice pistols you have there. I buy them from you for five hundred pesos."

JT told Villa, "I do not think I will be parting with them today at any price."

Villa wanted to say, "Maybe I kill you and take them from you," but in a moment of clarity, he saw it might not be a good idea; that they were all probably very good with their guns, and it would be him that would be shot and killed. Villa was determined to have those guns of JT's. Villa offered to put up any amount in a sharpshooting contest against his finest marksman for the Colt 44 pistols. JT knew he could win and was not concerned about losing. Villa told them to follow him to his camp just around the bend, which they had just left.

JT said in Spanish, "You want us to ride into the wolf's den."

Pancho Villa laughed and said, "If I am the Wolf then you, my friend, are the Tiger."

JT agreed, sensing this might be the only peaceful way to escape their situation. As they entered the camp JT asked his two companions to keep an eye on the Mexicans; they would shoot them all if given the chance. The Oklahoma ex-sheriff had been in similar situations many times and told JT not to worry; he had had him killed for over thirty minutes. That meant during their conversation, he had the drop on Villa. JT won the match and handed the man back his money. Villa insisted JT keep the money; that it was a fair match, but he would not.

After the match, the men sat around the camp talking as though they had been friends a long time. Villa had taken a liking to JT, and as JT and his companions were departing, Villa, going by the name Francisco, gave JT the address of a ranch that he could send word to in the event of any personal trouble in old Mexico.

My new friend is Pancho Villa!

About five years after Pancho Villa and JT's first visit in the mountains of Mexico, JT had established himself as a well-known breeder of thoroughbred horses and a wealthy mine owner. JT moved his family to Mexico while leaving his business headquarters in El Paso, Texas. A newspaper article dated July 1, 1906 reads, *American Horses to be bred on Mexican Range. Galena, State of Chihuahua, Mexico, June 30. The first attempt to breed thoroughbred horses on a large scale in Mexico is being made here by J. Todd McClammy, an American with years of experience in that business. He owns a ranch near Galena, which he is stocking with thoroughbred mares and stallions, which he bought in Kentucky and Tennessee. Mr. McClammy says that this high altitude and splendid climate is specially adapted to raising horses and he believes that his venture will be successful.*

JT liked to see his name in print. It made everything real to him. When the paper stated years earlier that he was a well-known cowboy and a wealthy miner, it became fact to those who did not know him because the newspaper said it was so. People who had never met JT respected him because of what they had read in the newspaper.

While JT became well known in America and Mexico as a horse breeder and a mine owner, Pancho Villa became well known as a Robin Hood bandit, stealing from the rich and giving to the poor peons. Pancho Villa had a gang of hundreds and was considered a hero to the peons.

While JT was leaving the local meat market in Galena the man next to him tying up his horse recognized JT and said, "It is the Tiger from the mountains with the nice pistols."

JT turned and said, "And you are the Wolf who wanted them."

"Yes, JT, it is me, Francisco. It has been a long time; what are you doing here?"

"I bought a ranch outside of town and raise thoroughbred horses and own a mine nearby."

Francisco said, "I am looking for fresh horses all the time. These thoroughbred horses are fast, yes?"

JT said, "Very fast."

Francisco said, "Maybe I will come visit your ranch and buy some of these horses."

JT said, "I have very nice quarter horses as well. Please come over for breakfast and meet my wife and children, and I can show you my horses." JT knew Julia would like to meet the man from the mountains that called him the Tiger.

Francisco Pancho Villa was hesitant to except the offer for breakfast because of the large reward of fifty thousand dollars on his head. Villa asked JT to wait one moment while he purchased something from the store. Villa asked the storeowner, who was actually Villa's brother about JT. His brother told Villa, "JT spends a lot of money in my store and treats me very well."

Villa accepted JT's invitation to breakfast. On the ride to JT's house, JT still did not know that he was riding with Pancho Villa, who called himself Francisco to JT.

Julia had already made breakfast while JT was at the store. JT brought Villa into their home and introduced him as Francisco, the man he had told Julia about, who called him the Tiger when he said they were riding into the Wolf's den. JT and Francisco told the story of how they met, while enjoying a very nice breakfast with the family.

After breakfast, JT showed Villa his horses. Villa was very impressed and told JT he will buy one hundred of his horses now and hundreds more soon. JT asked Francisco if he was going to start an army or something. Villa said, "Something like that. JT, you do not recognize me."

"Yes, Francisco, you are the man I met in the mountains who called me the Tiger and wanted my guns."

"Well, I still want your guns, and you're right; I am that man. I am also known as Pancho Villa."

"You're Pancho Villa? You do not look like your wanted poster. I have heard the stories of the great Robin Hood bandit, but no, I did not know it was you. Well it is nice to meet you Pancho Villa." JT told Villa he would be happy to sell him as many horses and supplies as he needed. He told Villa that he bought supplies from El Paso regularly and all he had to do was let him know ahead of time and he would be happy to fill his orders. JT felt a sense of adventure about his new friendship with Villa and let him know he was always welcome.

JT saw Villa looking at his Colt 44 pistols that he had wanted so badly. JT removed his pistols and holster and handed them to Villa. "Go ahead; put them on and fire as many rounds as you want."

Villa knew he had a trusted friend with this gesture. This friendship bonded with trust would last the rest of their lives. JT had read of the large reward on Villa's head and as Villa was getting ready to leave, JT asked Villa how he knew he could trust him.

"I went in the meat market where we met earlier

and asked the owner, who is also my brother. He said you were a man that could be trusted, and I believed him."

After Villa left, JT ran into the house and told Julia that his friend was actually Pancho Villa and he wanted to buy hundreds of horses. Julia told JT, "That is great; you go get 'em, Tiger."

A few weeks later, Villa invited JT to his wedding, where they danced and celebrated. Villa became a good friend of the family, as well as a good customer. Villa liked to talk to JT about matters. He felt JT had a good perspective on most things and respected his input.

JT told his friend Frank about Pancho Villa being the man called Francisco from the mountains and how he wanted to buy hundreds of horses from him. Frank did not share his enthusiasm and told JT that his involvement would be bad for business. Frank became a silent partner of JT's afterward and became more of a distant friend.

Here come the angels

Early morning in Galena Mexico as the sun would just start to rise was JT's favorite time to stroll around his ranch; everything was quiet and very peaceful. This particular morning he was down on the lower forty checking on a new colt. He was excited that this could be his best bred thoroughbred horse yet. He noticed his ranch hands were not up yet; he thought they probably played cards late and just were not awake. Suddenly, he heard the horses startled over something. There were about fifty horses on his range, and it sounded like someone was stealing them.

JT came out of the barn and surprised two federales. He shot and killed them and ran to the house, shooting at other federales on horses as he made his way to the house. Julia was awakened and heard the gunshots. She immediately broke out the rifles and laid them out on the table. The kids were grabbed out of their beds and brought into the dining room, where the rifles were spread out on the kitchen table. JT made his way back to the house and was very happy to see Julia had taken action. JT raised the kids with a stern hand, teaching them how to shoot a rifle and pistol as soon as they were strong enough to lift them. This is the way he was raised, and it saved him more than once.

JT put a rifle in Ila and Marvelle's hands, opened the windows, and told them to shoot at anything that moved. JT, Julia, the kids, two ranch hands and the cook were all that was left of the fifteen men working on the ranch. Everyone was shooting and the young boys were handing out bags of ammunition. This went on for about a half hour. The sun was rising, leaving the federales vulnerable. The federales pulled back and were going to try burning them out when Pancho Villa's men came riding in with about twenty men. They had always protected the ranch, but they were ambushed and many men were killed before Villa's men overtook the federales. One of Villa's men was caught the day before. He was tortured, and told the federales where the ranch was that supplied Villa's men with horses and supplies. Upon arriving at the ranch, Villa's men killed the federales as they were running towards the ranch house with torches trying to burn it down.

It was not long after that terrifying day that the Mexican President Porfirio Diaz took control of all property and declared it property of Mexico. This included all JT's mines and his ranch. JT was forced to move his family back to El Paso, Texas. JT took a huge loss. His mine he bought in 1906, as shown in a newspaper article, was doing very well. The Mexican Government had stolen from JT and this made him very angry. Villa's gang was hundreds and hundreds strong as they continued to steal from the federales and the rich to build their bandit gang into an army.

Candidate for President Francisco Madero was sympathetic toward the peons and told them when he was elected President he would give the land back to them. Madero would have won the election if not stopped by the corrupt government of Diaz, who did not intend to let Madero take office. Instead, they threw him in jail.

On October 5, 1910, Madero snuck out a letter from jail called "Plan de San Luis Potosi." Its slogan was "free suffrage and no re-election." Madero declared the Diaz government illegal and called on the Mexicans to rise up and overthrow the corrupt Diaz government. He soon escaped with the help of his father and made his way to San Antonio, Texas. Madero prepared a plan to overthrow the corrupt government of Diaz, and it included Pancho Villa, hero to the peons. A messenger immediately brought word of this to Villa's attention with a message inviting Villa to Madero's house. Villa took this as a great honor. Madero knew Villa was a great leader of the peons and invited him to be a general in his army against the corrupt government. Madero told Villa, "When we overthrow the corrupt Diaz government, I will take my rightful place as President and give the land back to the people."

Villa was extremely honored and rallied thousands of peons into his army. Villa tried very hard to be a good general, but it was hard to break from the ways of a bandit. History tells us of the revolution, the battles Pascual Orozco and Governor Abraham Gonzalez took in victory at Mexico City and Chihuahua City, but the story of how Villa quietly rode into town and overthrew the government without a gunshot has never been told until now.

Madero did not like Villa's ways and Villa very much wanted to impress Madero and hand him a victory. He had a plan, but to make it work would take the help of his old friend JT. He told his army to make camp on the Mexican side of the border as Villa and a dozen of his men rode to JT's house in El Paso to discuss his plan with JT. When they arrived at JT's house, it was late at night. Julia made Villa and JT some coffee and Villa told JT of his plan. Villa told JT his plan was to dress his daughters up as angels and ride right into town in a small caravan with his army not far behind. "The President loves gifts. We will put the guns in a basket and fill the rest of the basket with pastries and flowers, presented to him by two angels.

He will see this audience out of curiosity. No one will know what is happening, and we will walk right into city hall and raise our revolution flag, and kick their buts out of there. That is, with your permission, of course, Julia."

JT looked at Julia and said, "They have taken our property. We need to give assistance in overthrowing the corrupt Diaz government."

Julia looked at JT and Villa and told them, "If anything happens to our children, I will never forgive either one of you."

JT helped fine-tune the plan and expressed to Villa, "This crazy plan of yours is going to work."

Villa was very excited to move forward with the plan. Villa asked Julia if she could make a revolution flag. "We will raise it up high after we smash them like bugs."

Julia said to Villa with a big smile, "Yes, I will make the great General Francisco Pancho Villa a revolution flag."

Julia worked hard sewing through till morning. The flag was finished and the wings were attached to white dresses, which made the girls, Ila and Marvelle, look like angels. Julia wrapped the flag around John Junior, who they called Tolly, to sneak it across the border.

JT quickly had his ranch hands wake and ready the horses with supplies and weapons. He told them he would pay them well if they would join them on their journey. He did not want to scare them with the details at that time. By early morning, they were ready to ride out. Julia told JT, "Let's go get 'em, Tiger."

Villa knew of a cannon they could use and insisted they ride and pick it up. The caravan was packed with provisions and heavily armed. They were ready and anxious to carry out their plan.

The picture shown is of the cannon Pancho Villa insisted on getting and my Grandmother Marvelle and my Great Aunt Ila dressed up as angels, accompanied by JT, Pancho Villa and a caravan of a dozen on their way to overthrow the corrupt Mexican Government.

The picture shown is of Ila and Marvelle dressed as angels with Pancho Villa, accompanied by JT and a caravan of a dozen on their way to overthrow the corrupt Mexican Government.

By the time the caravan reached Ciudad Juarez, it was about mid-morning. Villa was not recognized at all riding with JT's family. Villa's army was staged just outside town. He had about a thousand soldiers. About eight hundred would be outside of town and two hundred would ride into town when given the signal. Soldiers were stretched out just within sight of each other, ready to convey the message to Villa's army, where a couple hundred soldiers were staged just outside of town. As they entered the town towards City Hall, they got a few strange looks but no one was the wiser about what was about to happen. They stopped in front of City Hall and a federale immediately approached them. "What is your business here?"

"We are traveling through. We were told the President is in town and we wanted to meet your great President. We bring gifts presented by angels."

The federale said, "Normally, the President does not take an audience without an appointment but I think he will want to see this."

Villa was dressed casually with a gentlemen's hat and is not recognized. The federale told the President of the strange travelers dressed as angels and bringing gifts. He told the President they looked harmless enough. The President told him, "How amusing. I must see this; bring them in."

The federale escorted them in to see the President. The signal was given to one of Villa's men down the street, who passed on the word man by man to the outside of town. The army started to surround the town without any resistance. The President was told that Villa and the other rebel generals' armies were far from the city and there was no immediate threat to Ciudad Juarez. JT, Villa, Ila, Marvelle and two ranch hands that were carrying the basket entered the President's chamber. The President laughed out loud, "Marvelous, two little angels bringing gifts."

"Yes, Mr. President, lovely flowers and pastries," the girls said as the men lowered the basket to the floor and quickly grabbed the guns. JT held the President at gunpoint and told the federales in the room to be quiet and not move or he would kill the President. The federales saw that it was not an exaggeration so they did exactly as they were told in hopes of saving the President's life.

The President asked, "What do you want? How long do think you can keep this up, with your two little angels with rifles. Even if you kill me, you will be dead before you can leave the building."

"No, I do not think so," Villa said as he lifted up his hat.

"Pancho Villa!"

"Yes Mr. Ex-President. You will stand down peacefully or I will execute you and your men." At that moment, Villa's men of about eight hundred surrounded the town and about two hundred surrounded City Hall. The President gave the word to stand down and to take no action. Villa announced his victory; Madero was now President of Mexico and the land once again belonged to the people. Villa immediately sent word to Madero and told him of the victory and that Mexico was waiting for their new President to arrive.

That evening, Pancho Villa put the revolution flag on top of a pole and drove it into the street. Villa addressed his special appointed solders. "This is our Revolution Flag, made by Mrs. Julia McClammy." Villa told the solders, "When the first shadow from the flag is cast by the morning sun, the contest will start. The first solider to win the race around town and gain control of the flag will be one of my generals in my army." The contest became a death battle. Before Villa could put a stop to the contest, one man was killed and the flag ripped in two.

The revolution years

After the victory of Ciudad Juarez, which overthrew Porfirio Diaz, General Victoriano Huerta appointed Pancho Villa chief military commander. Pancho Villa was now bigger than life. During the next couple of years, JT moved forward on his mining operations in Mexico, continued to breed his thoroughbred horses and sold real estate with his wife Julia.

Just as things were settling into a normal lifestyle, JT received word that Villa was arrested for keeping a horse that he had seized from a man. Huerta and Villa had been butting heads and Huerta used this as an excuse to do away with Villa once and for all. Huerta ordered Villa's execution for insubordination. President Madero's brother Raul intervened and Villa escaped across the border to JT's house, where he was given a warm welcome.

Villa was emotional with regret that he let down Madero and was a disgrace to all of Mexico. JT moved Villa to a room in town to give him space to work things out. Villa continued to wallow in self-pity and disgrace. Villa decided to go visit his compadre Carlos Jauregul in Havana to cheer him up. After hearing of Madero's assassination, Pancho Villa and Carlos Jauregul headed for El Paso, Texas, to meet up with his good friend JT McClammy. When he arrived at JT's house Villa said to JT, "My friend, my beloved President Madero is dead--will you help me revenge his death and join me in kicking Huerta's ass?"

JT said, "I knew you would be coming; fresh horses, guns, and ammunition, along with provisions, are ready to load up."

Villa said, "Thank you; you truly are one of my best friends."

Pancho Villa, when quoted a few years later in an article found in *The Sunday News Tribune,* Duluth, Minnesota July 2, 1916 best tells what happened next: *Carlos Jauregul and I left Havana two days after the news was received of Madero's assassination. We arrived in El Paso on March 1, 1913, and we stopped at the home of Todd McClammy, an American cowboy who is one of my best friends. On the night of the seventh day of March 1913, I at the head of nine brave men grasped destiny's firm hand and crossed the Rio Grande into Mexico. Each man was supplied with a horse, three guns, and all the ammunition he could carry besides a liberal quantity of coffee, frijoles and other provisions. Those who accompanied me on this benevolent enterprise were Juan Dozal, Manuel*

Ochoa, Daria Silva, Carlos Jauregui, Doctor Navarro, Manuel Medinabeytia and Todd McClammy. By July of that year, I had two thousand followers. Huerta began to realize that I had become a serious menace to his personal safety, so he quickly dispatched twelve hundred federales to San Andres under General Felix Terrazas to annihilate my army and make me prisoner. Instead of waiting for Terrazas to find me, I went out to look for Terrazas. His camp was asleep when we arrived. It was easy; we killed six hundred of them, captured four cannons, plenty of ammunition, 800 rifles and a great quantity of food and supplies. The rest of the federales scattered like whipped dogs before our wrath. Two weeks later a letter arrived in my camp. General Carranza was declaring himself head of the new revolution against Huerta and invited me to join his banner. 'Anything to avenge Madero,' I replied. I am at your orders. Three days after Carranza's note came, I led my army toward Jimenez, south of Chihuahua City, and in this town, others joined me. I made each leader a general and my army swelled to six thousand braves. Think of it, six thousand armed and mounted soldiers in as many months. And I started with nothing. Ah, it was a sad day for Huerta when I decided to crush him as I would a jumping tarantula.

The picture on the front cover has been blown up to show where a bullet had grazed his forehead. You can see JT in the group, at the "Last Victory," historically known as the "Constitutionalist Revolution of Mexico."

In this picture at the "Last Victory," Pancho Vila is holding JT's son William's hand. The battle became known as the "Constitutionalist Revolution of Mexico." Villa's army was known as "Villa's Division del Norte" (Northern Division). This was the last victory for Pancho Villa. JT noted this in his photo album, calling it the "Last Victory."

One of the most interesting events that transpired on Villa and Carranza's journey to crush Huerta was the train robbery. Villa had learned of a shipment of silver bullion worth approximately $50,000 from a Wells Fargo agent who was sympathetic to their cause and wanted to help. The train was easily robbed and the silver bars confiscated. The $50,000 would be enough to finance their army. The only problem was they could not spend the silver bars. They needed cash. The plan that was offered by the Wells Fargo agent was to ransom the silver and himself for a $50,000 cash payment and safe passage for Wells Fargo in the future.

Wells Fargo nicely documented the events that took place during the negotiations. The documents were purchased by the University of California, Berkeley, and are now available for public viewing. The first letter notifies Wells Fargo's head office of the train robbery and the stolen silver bars. A detailed letter describes the contents of the silver bullion stolen, right down to the size and weight of each bar. The negotiations of the ransom become known as the "Hush-Hush Deal." The letters and telegrams were encoded for secrecy. The solved codes with the real messages are included in the collection of letters owned by the University of California, Berkeley. With the negotiating skills of JT for Villa's interest, the exchange of the silver bars for cash, the Wells Fargo agent and safe passage eventually takes place without public knowledge. It truly was a "Hush-Hush Deal."

This picture was taken by JT during the exchange of silver bars to U.S. currency. Wells Fargo agents and Pancho Villa's chief officers, shown in front, conducted the transaction.

The attempt to assassinate Villa was found in a newspaper article in the *Lima Daily News*. Headlines read *Lima Ohio Wednesday, February 18, 1914. Plot against Villa. Juarez, Mexico, Several constitutionalist army officers were arrested today, charged with being implicated in a plot to assassinate General Francisco Villa at the Constitutionalist Commandery. Two reports were current: One included the name of Luis Terrazas, whose father's estate was seized by Villa; the other brought the name of General Venustiano. It was said that one of the prisoners made a confession that a bomb was to be placed under the house Villa occupied in Juarez. The assassin was then to escape in an automobile and to receive $150,000 if the plot was successful. For some time there have been reports of strained relations between Villa and Carranza, and it has been said that Villa feared to go south with his army for fear that Carranza would take possession of all the authority Villa had acquired in northern Mexico. Today, however, was the first time that actual hostility between the two men has been spoken of. The plot against Villa's life is said to have been discovered by John Todd McClammy, American head of Villa's secret police. The prisoners are being closely guarded and probably will be court-martialed and secretly shot. Picked troops have been placed around Villa's house* as a guard. *Villa, who has been in the habit of passing the evenings in the gambling halls of Juarez, has been cautioned to remain indoors at night.*

One year later, as noted in the *Reno Evening Gazette* on Tuesday, August 18, 1914, was the biggest roundup of cattle in all of history. Four hundred thousand cattle were sold for a profit of eight million dollars. This was split between Don Luis and Pancho Villa. Villa's half would go to supporting the new order of things in northern Mexico. JT was paid a very nice sum for his help in making the roundup come together with his well-known drover skills.

This article in *The Dallas Morning News*, Dallas Texas, Sunday July 2, 1916, shows JT purchasing an ore mine that generated large profits. It reads as follows: *El Pasoans interested in providence mines. Rich deposits of copper ore in Jarilla Mountains. El Paso, Texas June 30, El Paso capital is extensively interested in the Providence copper mine, about fifty miles from El Paso in Jarilla Mountains, which are noted for the ore that they have yielded. The Providence mine was founded sometime in the 1880s by Billy Gibbs, a prospector from St. Louis, and was later patented by St. Louis capital. After being transferred through a chain of capitalists including C. C. Carroll and F. G. Smith, it finally finds its way in the hands of J. Todd*

McClammy of El Paso. At first McClammy only bought out the lease option, but finding the mine would yield a great profit in the future he bought the interest of his two partners Christian and Wasson for $10,000 and then began to make modern improvements. Carroll, who had in the meantime kept hold on his share, finally decided to sell out to McClammy. In May, 1915 McClammy found himself the sole owner of one of the largest growing copper mines in the Southwest. Barely, three months passed before McClammy found that his theory was right. The mine began to make big commercial shipments of the ore and made large profits.

With his mine doing so well, JT and Julia decided to end their ties with the Revolution and enjoy a more pleasant life in sunny California. The McClammys packed up and moved to Glendale, California in the beautiful San Fernando Valley.

Before leaving El Paso, JT met with Villa, letting him know of their move to California. JT told Villa he was ready to retire from the revolution and enjoy the rest of his life in sunny California. Villa understood and thanked JT for all his help over the years. Villa asked JT what he is going to do about horses and supplies. JT reminded him that he was the great Pancho Villa and he would figure it out. JT told Villa when he was ready to retire to come visit him in California.

Only a short time passed before JT read in his morning paper of Villa's attack on Columbus, New Mexico on March 9, 1916. Without JT's help with horses and supplies, the Americans swindled Villa. Villa's anger, fueled with vengeance, fired up his men, who were tempered in their ways from years of battles. Villa had no plan, only to attack and kill the men who sold him bad ammunition.

Villa and his men crossed the border of the United States into Columbus, New Mexico on their way to battle, as they had done so many times before. Villa had no control over his men once they went into battle mode. Villa's army went on a rampage, shooting and destroying everything in sight. What started out as revenge towards the ones who had sold them bad ammunition turned into a killing rampage on the town of Columbus, New Mexico. Unlike in Mexico, the Americans were better armed and supplied. This attack was exactly why the second amendment, giving the right to bear arms, was written into the constitution. The citizens of the United States were being attacked and they were pissed. The people of Columbus, New Mexico fought back with everything they had. In the end close to a hundred of Villa's men were killed, along with eighteen Americans.

After the attack the Americans, through the political push of the Hearst newspaper, demanded retribution against Pancho Villa. Under pressure to respond, U.S. President Wilson sent General Pershing and 10,000 troops to bring Pancho Villa to justice. After Villa's rage had cooled a bit, he realized his attack towards the men who sold him bad ammunition, which turned into a bloody mess, was a big mistake. Villa knew they would be coming after him. Villa's first instinct was to head for the high mountains where he had hid out in the past. After hiding out for a couple of months, Villa knew he would be caught if he stayed in the same location. Villa had seen airplanes and automobiles looking for him and knew he had to come up with a plan.

He had used disguises before and rode right through towns without being noticed, and that is what he would do this time. The only place he could think of going was JT's house in California. When he arrived in Glendale, California at the McClammy residence, he explained to JT how things went terribly wrong. His intensions were never to kill innocent people. Villa explained to JT that he could not control his men, and if he could take it back, he would.

JT was waiting for Villa to blame him for not being there to supply him with supplies he needed, but he never did. JT knew how Villa acted when he was angry. Villa acted on his anger without thinking things through. JT told Villa that he really made a mess of things this time. "If you are going to stay here, you will need to use a different name and clean up a bit."

Villa was clean-shaven and dressed in nice clothes. He was introduced as Francisco, a friend from Mexico. Villa stayed with the McClammys and was made to feel like part of the family. During evening conversation between JT and Villa, Villa told JT the whereabouts of his buried treasure, worth millions. Villa told JT if he could help him get it out of Mexico to the United States, he would split it with him.

JT told Villa this would take some doing, and that he knew exactly who to have help him on this endeavor. JT told Villa he would contact his friend and associate Dr. Frederick V. Ellis, and they would start planning their trip immediately.

After a year of pursuing Pancho Villa, President Wilson recalled General Pershing and gave him a command of the American Expeditionary Force in World War One. The unsuccessful pursuit to capture Pancho Villa came to be known as the Punitive Expedition. With the hunt for Pancho Villa over, Villa was free to return to Mexico and continue with his Revolution.

This newspaper article was found in the

Cumberland Evening Times Friday, November 7, 1919. This is a very interesting article telling of Villa's buried treasure that he could not spend and how JT helped Villa with a mining project to support his cause. The article reads as follows: *Rich, but he cannot collect. Poor Ellis! He owns Villa's Treasure! Movies May Aid. "We daren't touch it," Film Pioneer Tells his Interviewer. Spokane Washington November 7, knowledge of the location of millions of dollars worth of buried bullion. Money and Equipment to finance an expedition. Consent of the owner of the bullion. All that is his but he cannot touch the treasure! And it is turning the hair of Dr. Frederick V. Ellis from brown to grey. Back in the fastness of the hills of Chihuahua and Sonora Mexico, Pancho Villa's loot is buried. Some of it is in silver bullion; more is in gold bars almost too heavy for a man to lift. In caches here and there known only to himself and a few of his trusted lieutenants, the bandit supreme of the twentieth century has hidden his wealth. "Villa'd Divvy," if they could collect. Ravaged from rich haciendas at gunpoint, taken in swooping raids on isolated towns, captured after fierce desert battles with Carrancista troops, this loot, the savings of years of banditry, General Villa would gladly divide with Americans if the Americans could get it out of Mexico. Villa's wealth is all dressed up and no place to go. He* *wants supplies, guns, shells, and airplanes. He cannot buy them in Mexico. Neither can he get his money out and purchase his needs in America. Although a few Americans in Villa's confidence know the location of some of his wealth, they dare not try to get it to the American side. It is practically down to the last peso, stolen property. "I might get over a thousand pounds or so," says Doctor Ellis, "and I might with luck repeat the performance, but United States Secret Service men would be on my trail before long and between wealth and freedom, give me freedom." Villa's mine soon to start production. Villa, however, intends to start production again on his placer mine in Chihuahua. Legitimate profits from this mine the bandit can spend to arm and equip his troops. In a letter to J. Todd McClammy of El Paso, Texas, Villa asks for McClammy's aid in this project. "It is a wonderfully rich mine." Ellis, who is an associate of McClammy, says "Some time ago Villa's men worked at it for 14 days. They took out $18,000. Then the Carrancistas came along, captured the mine and shut Villa out." The bandit now is seeking through his American agents, American aid in reopening the workings. Ellis and McClammy are perfectly willing to help in this meritorious enterprise, but they daren't. However, Ellis is a pioneer in the motion picture business. He* *is getting together a company of actors and actresses. They are going down into the deserts and mountains of Sonora and film Villa in his lair. Ellis denies the motion picture enterprise has any relation to the buried treasure. But strange things happen down in Manana land. Curious tales seep through the border. Silent little parties sometimes slip over the Rio Grande on moonless nights. "We daren't touch it," Ellis repeats.*

History recorded the long hard times of the Mexican Revolution through hundreds of newspaper articles covering Pancho Villa on a daily basis. The press had a field day with every battle, which was covered colorfully throughout the Revolution. JT's involvement was very seldom found in the newspapers, although JT was by Villa's side through some of the toughest battles. The articles found show a friendship and trust that JT and Villa had in each other, one that molded them into who they were during these tough revolution years.

The last chapter

The McClammy family was very happy living in Glendale, California in the beautiful San Fernando Valley. The warmer climate was appealing to JT, and this is where he would make his residence for his remaining years. Before 1920, JT had acquired enough wealth to retire and escape the financial ruin of the country, known today as the Great Depression. Julia and JT enjoyed selling real estate and staying active.

His boys had become known as the bad boys of Glendale. Their mannerisms seemed quite normal to them but did not quite fit in with the upscale community they were now living in. One of their friends who liked to hang out and play cowboys and Indians was a boy named Marion Morrison, who we all know as John Wayne.

One day around 1916-1917, while going through some of his things, JT came across the sheriff's badge that was given to him by Sheriff Tom Clary. JT's son George was nearby and saw the sheriff badge shining in the light, he ran to his dad and asked him about it. JT told his son about how he obtained the badge and captured the bad man Murphy.

After hearing the story, George asked his dad

if he could wear the sheriff's badge when they played cowboys and Indians. JT stared at the badge for a while, recalling memories of his father and the capture of Murphy. He looked at his youngest son George, pinned the sheriff badge on him, and said, "There's a new sheriff in town."

From that day on, JT called his son George the sheriff. When my Dad was growing up, his Grandpa John (JT) called him the sheriff. Years later, my Dad liked to call his grandsons sheriff. It must have been the feeling of the Old West glory days, brought on from his sons and daughters having ranch style homes with horses that surfaced those memories that my Dad wanted to pass on.

The McClammy Boys, William, John, and George.

"The Bad boys of Glendale."

In 1920, Villa was asked to retire or face exile. The terms were negotiated by Villa's oldest and most trusted friend, JT. The Mexican government was anxious to move forward without the influence Pancho Villa still had with the people of Mexico. For the total removal of Villa's involvement in any government status and for him to retire quietly, JT was able to negotiate a settlement of $5,000,000 and 650,000 acres of land.

After the negotiations Villa was grateful for JT's help and told JT, "If there is anything I can give you let me know and it is yours."

JT mentioned land on the Mexican coast that he had been eyeing for years. He told Villa that it would be a wonderful place to retire. Villa was very happy to be able to do this for his old friend JT. Soon after Villa was settled into his retirement and sent word requesting a visit from his old friend JT.

JT made the trip to visit Villa at his big ranch in Canutillo Durango. When JT arrived at the ranch, it was apparent that Villa was not exactly retiring peacefully. Villa's army of over a hundred men covered the grounds. JT knew Villa was up to something. Villa told JT these men were there to protect him against assassination attempts. Villa took JT to his retirement home at the Constitutionalist

Commandery for a more pleasant visit. The picture shown is of Villa and JT on that visit.

Villa wanted to know how JT was, and surprised him with a note for 100,000 acres on the Mexican coast. Villa always said he would repay JT for his trustworthiness as head of his secret service and for repeatedly saving his life. JT accepted the note for the property and told Villa that it was an honor being the good friend of the great Pancho Villa. This was the last time JT was to see his long time friend, Pancho Villa. Pancho Villa was assassinated on July 20, 1923.

JT and Pancho Villa at Villa's retirement home,
the Constitutionalist Commandery.

The *Helena Daily Independent* newspaper ran an article on April 10, 1927 with the headline *Finds his paradise, buys 1,000 acres, and is located for life.* The article reads as follows: *San Diego, April 9, all his long and eventful life, Todd McClammy, old-time cattleman and soldier of fortune, has been in search of paradise. Several times, he has thought that he was about to make the discovery with the assistance of opponents' six-shooters. But now he has found it, and it is not in Heaven at all; it is down in the Tepic valley in the state of Nayarit, on the west coast of Mexico. There, according to McClammy, lies everything that a man in his most imaginative moments could ask for. Bananas, coffee, sugar cane, avocados, citrus fruits--in fact, all kinds of fruits, vegetables and cereals grow there abundantly, he says. Its climate is the most equable to be found, varying only 10 degrees. Because of the altitude, the valley is 4,000 feet above sea level. It never grows hot and because of the influence of the sea breeze and its geographical location, it never gets cold. And best of all it has an average rainfall of 40 inches a year, which makes irrigation unnecessary. So impressed was he with the spot that he has purchased 100,000 acres in the valley, which he and his sons intend to farm, he said. Parts are to be planted to sugar cane, part to citrus fruits and part to avocados. Mr. McClammy*

*was a cattleman in the days when cattle were driven
in herds from Texas to Montana and Canada and he
made the trip over the old Chisholm trail with herds six
times. The average time for the trip was nine months,
but once it took eleven months, he said.*

For some reason, his plan to move his family to
the Tepic Valley on the coast of Mexico did not pan out.
My guess would be that the note Villa had given JT
for the property was null and void after Villa's death.
JT's family remained in Glendale, California, enjoying
a more relaxed lifestyle.

Many years later JT read a newspaper article,
found in the *Helena Daily Independent*, dated February
16, 1939. The article was about an old artist friend of
JT's, Charles Russell, who he had played poker with
on many occasions back in the day. The headline read
Story of Russell Painting of lassoed bear related. JT
had not thought of the story about the bear and his
brother in many years. The story tells of the killing
of the bear painted by Charles M. Russell around
1914. A ferocious cinnamon bear weighing about
700 pounds had entered the D.H.S. and Square outfit
camp. The bear had come in at night and killed some
of their horses. The next morning riders set out to kill
the bear. Among the riders was JT's brother, Quincy
McClammy.

After reading the article, JT realized it had been a very long time since he had seen his brothers. William and Quincy were both in World War One as shown by their draft registration cards, 1917-1918. JT had visited his brothers a few years after they returned home from World War One, around 1926. He decided to visit his brothers and bring his sister Bettie Boone, who had not seen her brothers in about forty years. Both JT's brothers William and Quincy had married Indian women of the Sioux Assiniboine tribe of the Fort Peck Reservation in the Oswego valley of Montana. Both of his brothers had very large families. William and his wife Phillipena lived in Poplar, Roosevelt, Montana and Quincy and his wife Minnie lived in Oswego Valley, Montana. They had a jim-dandy of a visit and returned to Southern California, where JT had become accustomed to the warmer weather.

While in Montana visiting his brothers, with his sister, JT gave a last interview to *The Poplar Standard* in Poplar Montana on September 5, 1940. This article substantiates many facts throughout the book and is used as a focal point for the countless hours of research. Many quotes and phrases are taken directly from this article in an effort to make the stories as authentic as possible. The writer of this article changed events slightly to accommodate the readers and possibly the editor. Some of the actual events that were uncovered in the lengthy research process are slightly unpleasant, as well as hard to believe. Overall, it is a very well done article, considering the wild stories that came from a 71-year-old cowboy, from a time most people had forgotten about.

The article headline reads *John T. (Todd) McClammy Tells of Early Day Experiences in Montana and Old Mexico*. The article reads as follows: *John T. (Todd) McClammy and sister, Mrs. Boone who live in California, are visiting at the home of their brother, William, in Poplar. This is the first time in 40 years that Mrs. Boone had seen her brother here, John having visited in Poplar in 1926. They also visited another brother, Q. McClammy at Oswego.*

During his visit here, Mr. McClammy called at the Standard office and was kind enough to grant an interview to tell of his many thrilling experiences in pioneer Montana days and in Old Mexico. Mr. McClammy first came to this part of the country in 1884, helping drive a herd of cattle up from Texas on the Famous Chisholm trail, named after John Chisholm, one of the first cattlemen to drive stock this far north. He made six of these trips, each of which took from nine to eleven months and he said the herds ranged in size from 3,000 to 5,000 head.

In 1888, he was made manager of the Bar-11 ranch, and made his home near what is now the town of Shelby. In his interesting manner, he related a thrilling experience while at Shelby when that entire section was out to capture, dead or alive, a western bad man by the name of Frank Murphy. Murphy, who was wanted for several murders and horse thefts, was known to be in that neighborhood and posses were hastily organized to take after him. McClammy was asked to join one of these but figured that they already had more men then were needed.

One night, while he was in his hotel room in Shelby, he was awakened by the telegraph operator who advised him that he had received a wire from the depot agent at Conrad saying that Murphy had just killed a man there and was headed for a nearby construction camp. Conrad at that time was just a coal chute and had a boxcar depot. McClammy immediately sent the operator to the hardware store for a supply of 30-30 shells while he dressed. He rushed through this procedure in time to catch a freight train out of Shelby to Conrad, which he reached several hours later.

Here McClammy learned the details of the cold-blooded murder. Murphy, whose horse had played out, had turned the animal loose a short distance from Conrad and had hid his saddle in a coulee. While in

Conrad, a cowboy, completely outfitted even to a six-shooter, approached Murphy. The outlaw, seeing the man and mistaking him for an officer of the law, shot him through the head without warning. The victim was known only by the name of Klondike.

McClammy, figuring that the murderer would head for the construction camp to obtain a fresh horse, started in pursuit. McClammy captured the outlaw in the cook tent where he was trying to force a Negro cook to steal the foreman's horse from him. McClammy said that as he threw down with his rifle on Murphy, the colored cook cut a hole in the tent with a butcher knife and headed out across the country. Murphy was bound and taken to Fort Benton where he was turned over to Tom Clary, who was sheriff of the county at the time. For his brave deed, Clary gave McClammy two specially made single action frontier model Colt 44 pistols.

McClammy met the famous Mexican Pancho Villa while showing two men, one an ex-U.S. Marshal and the other an Oklahoma ex sheriff, land that could be purchased for a cattle ranch. Villa and two companions came into McClammy camp and the fine pistols worn by McClammy almost immediately attracted the big revolutionist. When Villa offered McClammy 500 pesos (Mexican dollars) for the weapons, McClammy said he would not part with it at any price. Although neither McClammy nor his partners knew that their visitor was the most hunted outlaw in Mexico with a price of $50,000 on his head, they did realize that they were in the tightest spot that any of the three had previously been in. At that time, this section of Old Mexico was infested with many ruthless and cold-blooded outlaws.

Upon McClammy's refusal to sell the weapons, Villa, noted as a pistol marksman, offered to put up any amount of money against the McClammy gun in a target shooting contest. It was a bet, Villa putting up 500 pesos against the pistol. Just before the contest started, McClammy warned his two companions to keep an eye on the Mexicans, that they might shoot all of them if given the opportunity. The Oklahoma ex-sheriff, who saw something very familiar about the situation, told McClammy, "Don't worry, I've had him killed for over 30 minutes," meaning that during the conversation, the Oklahoma ex-sheriff had the drop on Villa.

McClammy won in a fair match. McClammy was an outstanding marksman at that time and felt confident of winning the match. Following the display of marksmanship, the men all sat around and visited in a most friendly manner. Villa took a liking to McClammy and gave him the address of a ranch where, in the event of any future personal trouble in Old Mexico, he could send word and get the help he needed at any time. Villa did not reveal his identity. Soon after this adventure, McClammy, moved with his family from El Paso, Texas, to Chihuahua, Mexico with the capital of the same name.

It was five years later, just as McClammy was leaving the meat market one morning that he met Villa again. Pancho was very pleased to see his old friend from the mountains, as he called McClammy. Almost his first question concerned the beloved weapons he had tried so hard to acquire. McClammy said he still possessed the weapons and invited Villa to have breakfast with him at his home and to meet Mrs. McClammy and the children. Villa, thinking of the large reward offered for his capture, was slow to accept the invitation, but after consulting with the proprietor of the meat market, he went along with to the McClammy home. Later, McClammy learned that the butcher was Pancho's brother.

At this time McClammy, with a gesture of true old time frontiersman, took the coveted pistols, with its holster and full cartridge belt, and strapped them around Villa's waist. This act was to seal a lifelong friendship between the two men. McClammy was still in the dark as to the identity of his strange friend.

In 1910, Villa joined Francisco I. Madero in the Madero revolution. It was at this time, with the Mexicans camped just across the Rio Grande in Mexico, that McClammy smuggled the revolutionists their first flag. It had been made by Mrs. McClammy and was taken across the border wrapped around the body of McClammy's son, Tolly, who at the time was about five years of age. The flag was given to Villa, at that time, a Captain in Madero's small army. The flag caused more than a little commotion, as every officer in the group figured it should be his. One man lost his life when trying to gain possession of it, tearing it into two. Another man was shot and one drowned before the uprising was squelched.

A week or two after this incident, McClammy was invited to Villa's wedding at San Andreus, Pancho's hometown which is located 50 miles from Chihuahua. Following the wedding, Villa and McClammy loaded their saddle horses in a boxcar and hauled them to within seven miles of Chihuahua. They rode into town and took in a dance that was in progress at the time. They danced all night in the town crowded with the same men they were after. The next morning, Villa cashed a check for $14,000 that he gave to McClammy for the purchase of army provisions.

It was while getting these supplies that McClammy contacted many of the regulars of the Mexican army, many of who were in sympathy with the Villa cause. He told them they were surrounded and were fighting a hopeless issue. To avoid needless bloodshed, he advised them to give up. The result of these negotiations was that Villa made the capture of the town and the regular forces without the expedient of firing a shot. McClammy and Villa continued to be the best of friends, and McClammy was Pancho's representative in his largest and final deal with the Mexican government. This involved the turning over to Villa of 650,000 acres of ranch land and $5,000,000 in cash.

McClammy was associated with Villa almost until the time of his assassination and can describe this event and give names of the five men in the automobile when Pancho was killed. Mr. McClammy's story of the events of the early days could fill a book, far surpassing in interest other narratives of that period in history. He is one of the most interesting men we have had the privilege of talking to. His facts are clear as to intimate detail and follow a well-connected sequence that brings the story to life. An outstanding feature of this story is the fact that he can remember the first names and family titles of all of the officers with whom he came into contact. Our only regret is that we did not have the opportunity to meet Mr. McClammy sooner and have more time to devote to the interview.

JT liked to shoot birds with his long-time friend E.W. Mead, who was the general manager of the Sierra Madre Company.

JT and his friend E. W. Mead; a good day of shooting.

Not too many years later, JT moved himself into a retirement home so that he would not be a burden to anyone. JT always wore his famous Colt 44 pistols that Pancho Villa wanted so badly. When JT died in his retirement home on September 5, 1947, his famous pistols were stolen before any family members could claim them.

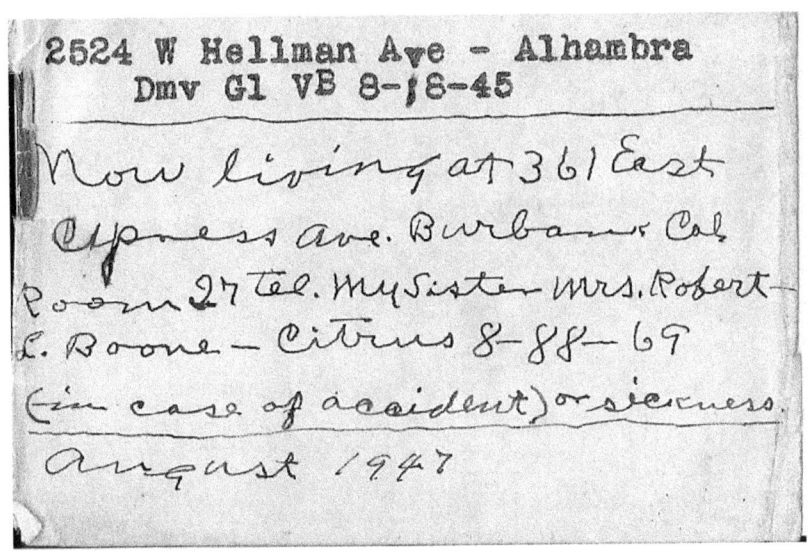

Back of JT's driver's license.

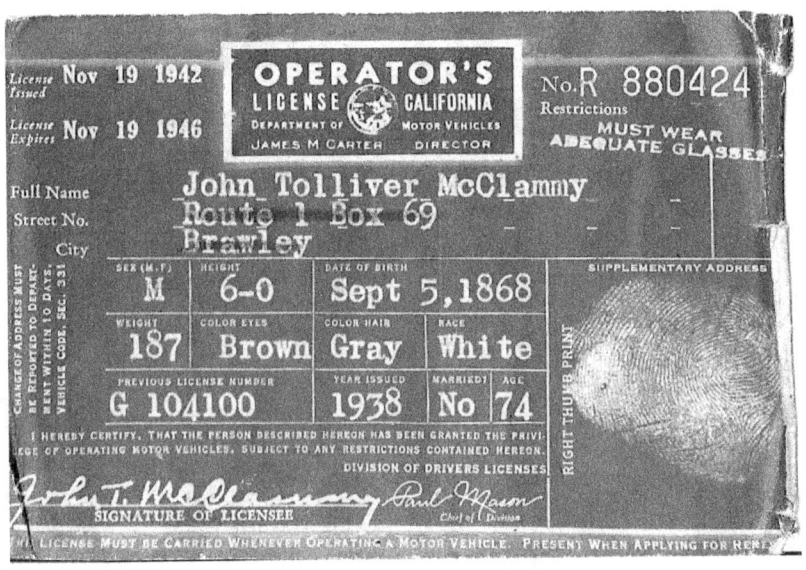

Front of JT's driver's license.

JT riding to the pearly gates.

www.pkhpublishing.com